MEET THE GIRL TALK CHARACTERS

Sabrina Wells is petite, with curly auburn hair, sparkling hazel eyes, and a bubbly personality. Sabrina loves magazines, shopping, sleepovers, and most of all, she loves talking to her best friends.

Katie Campbell is a straight-A student and super athlete. With her blond hair, blue eyes, and matching clothes, she's everyone's idea of little miss perfect. But Katie has a few surprises for everyone, including herself!

Randy Zak has just moved to Acorn Falls from New York City, and is she ever cool! With her radical spiked haircut and her hip New York clothes, Randy teaches everyone just how much fun it is to be different.

Allison Cloud is a Native American Indian. Allison's super smart and really beautiful. But she has one major problem: She's thirteen years old, five foot seven, and still growing!

Here's what they're talking about in
Girl Talk

RANDY: Hi, Katie. How ya' doing? You must be going crazy with all the plans for your mom's wedding.

KATIE: You're not kidding! Everytime I turn around mom has something else for me to do.

RANDY: It must be hard to deal with your mom getting remarried.

KATIE: It sure is, but it's really weird to think I'm going to have a whole new family — including a step-brother!

RANDY: Don't worry, Katie. I'm sure everything's going to turn out just fine.

KATIE: I sure hope you're right about this one, Ran!

HERE COMES THE BRIDE

By L. E. Blair

GIRL TALK® series created by Western Publishing Company, Inc.

Produced by Angel Entertainment, Inc.

Western Publishing Company, Inc., Racine, Wisconsin 53404

Text by: Leah Jerome

Chapter One

"K.C.!" I heard someone call out from behind me as I walked into the cafeteria for lunch on Wednesday. "K.C., over here!"

Without turning around, I knew it was Michel Beauvais. He's the only French Canadian at Bradley Junior High, and he speaks with an accent, so his voice is really easy to recognize, even in a noisy, crowded room. Also, Michel and my other teammates on the ice hockey team are the only people I know who call me K.C., instead of Katie.

I spotted his orange-and-black hockey jacket in a second and walked over to the table where he was sitting.

"*Ça va*? How are you, K.C.?" Michel asked, his eyes crinkling at the corners as he smiled.

His eyes are so dark they're almost the same color as his black hair. A lot of girls at Bradley think Michel is super-cute. I guess I just think of him as a teammate.

"*Ça va bien*," I replied, grinning at him. I had picked up quite a few French expressions from Michel — like this one, to tell him everything was fine. He kept telling me he couldn't believe how fast I was learning.

"Are you coming to the conditioning meeting today?" Michel wanted to know. Coach Budd was going to give us exercises to do in the off-season, so we wouldn't be totally out of shape when next season began. It sounded like a good idea to me.

I nodded. "Definitely," I replied. "I've got a lot of work to do if I want to make All-County next year."

"You'll make it," Scottie Silver said as he came up behind me. Scottie is the captain of the hockey team, and I have to say he's very cute. He's got curly blond hair and really blue eyes. "You're going to be the best left-winger in the league," Scottie went on. He tugged on my long blond ponytail and then sat down next to Michel.

It felt good to hear that from the captain of our team. I really love playing hockey. I guess that's something I inherited from my dad. He played semipro when he was young, and he taught me everything about the game. We used to spend a lot of time on the ice before he died.

Anyway, Bradley doesn't have a girls' hockey team, so I tried out for the boys' team last season and made it. Being on an all-boys team was kind of weird at first. All the guys had problems with a girl playing hockey. Of course, that was before I became the second-highest scorer on the team — right behind Scottie.

Now I think they sort of forget I'm a girl once we get out on the ice.

"I guess you're not going to be eating with us today, huh, K.C.?" Michel asked, breaking into my thoughts. Scottie looked up from the huge hero sandwich he was about to bite into. "As usual," he said, rolling his eyes.

"Come on, guys," I protested, holding up my hands. The whole hockey team eats together every day, except for me. They know I always eat with my best friends, but they like to give me a hard time. I looked around the cafeteria for Sabrina Wells and my two other best friends, Allison Cloud and Randy Zak. I hoped that one of them had gotten to lunch early and found a table, because the place was getting more and more crowded by the second.

Finally I spotted Randy and Al on the other side of the room. "I've got to go," I told my teammates, starting to walk away. "I'll talk to you guys after school."

"And I'll see you tonight, right, K.C.?" Michel asked. I paused and looked back at him.

"What's tonight?" I wanted to know, drawing a total blank.

"Dinner," Michel replied. "You know, my father, your mother."

"Oh, that's right," I said. My older sister, Emily, my mom, and I were going out with Michel and his father, who is named Jean-Paul.

"See you then," I said over my shoulder to Michel as I made my way over to where my friends were sitting. I thought about how my mom had started dating Michel's father a while back.

At first I thought the whole thing was really weird. I mean, my dad had died just three years ago, and I couldn't get used to the fact that my mom was dating. But I feel a lot better about it all now. And Mr. Beauvais is really cool.

"Hi, guys," I said when I reached my friends, sliding into a seat next to Allison.

"Hi, Katie," Al said, smiling at me. Al is Native American. She is really tall and really beautiful. She also has the most amazing long black hair. Today she was wearing overalls and a red knit shirt.

My other best friend, Randy Zak, finished taking a bite of her apple and asked, "What's going on, Katie?"

"Not too much," I said, pulling my turkey sandwich out of my lunch bag. Anyone looking at Randy and me would probably never guess that we are friends.

Randy moved here to Acorn Falls, Minnesota, at the beginning of the school year. She looks and dresses totally different from me, but she looks really cool. She has long black hair that's spiked on top, and she wears these wild clothes. Today she had on a green Day-Glo minidress that flared out at the bottom, black stockings, and black flats. She looked great, but I have to say, my style is totally different. More all-American or something. I was wearing blue jeans, a pink oxford shirt my mom had bought me, and a pink ribbon around my blond ponytail.

Suddenly we heard our friend Sabrina Wells

come up and exclaim, "Guys!" Then she plopped down at our table next to Randy. Her long, curly red hair bounced as she hit the chair, and her jumper was like a blue blur, billowing around her. For a person who's not even five feet tall, Sabs packs a lot of energy.

"You won't believe it!" she said.

"What?" Randy asked.

"Guess who's planning the seventh-grade class dance?"

"Who?" Allison asked, taking a bag of her grandmother's homemade oatmeal cookies from her lunch bag and handing them around. Sabs looked from Randy to Al to me before exclaiming, "Winslow!"

"Winslow?" I asked in surprise, speaking through a mouthful of cookie. Winslow Barton is the class brain. I really respect him, but I never would have thought of him as the class dance type. He's so serious, and everything he does is based on probabilities and statistics and all. Once we were partners in our health class when we had to be parents to an egg. Winslow almost drove me nuts with all of his charts and schedules.

"Yeah," Sabs confirmed. "He was one of

eight people who volunteered to be chairperson at the meeting, and I figured that the fairest way to choose would be to pick a name out of a hat."

Since Sabrina is president of the seventh-grade class, it's her job to pick the organizing committee for dances and stuff like that.

"So, what's Winslow going to do for the dance?" Randy asked.

"This is what you're not going to believe," Sabs said, pausing dramatically. "He called the newspaper and got all the data on what the current trends are. And he said, 'Based on the statistics, it appears that the decade of the 1960s has increased in popularity significantly over the last few months.'"

"Sabs is a great mimic. She sounded just like Winslow. We all started cracking up. I laughed so hard I was crying.

"So, am I to assume that we're having a sixties theme dance?" Randy asked after we had all gotten control of ourselves. Sabs nodded.

"Doesn't it sound awesome? I wonder if my mom has some bell-bottoms or anything groovy like that in the attic."

"I've got a great minidress!" Randy exclaimed. "It'll be perfect. What are you two going to wear?" she asked, turning to Al and me. Al and I looked at each other.

"I don't know," I admitted. "I don't think my mom was exactly the bell-bottom or miniskirt type." I giggled, totally unable to picture my mother in anything slightly resembling a miniskirt. Her skirts always reach below the knee.

Al munched thoughtfully on a cookie, then said, "I'm sure my mother doesn't have anything like that."

"Don't worry, we'll find something for both of you to wear," Randy told Al and me. Just then the warning bell rang, signaling the end of lunch period. "We'd better motor," Randy said. "We don't want to be late."

"Hey, are you guys coming over tonight to study for that math test tomorrow?" Sabs asked as we all stood up.

Shaking my head, I told her, "I can't. We're all going out to dinner with Jean-Paul and Michel."

"You guys are all going out together?" Randy asked, raising one eyebrow. I nodded, wondering why she thought that was weird. I mean, my mom and Jean-Paul go out a lot together. Michel and I don't go out with them that often, but so what?

"They've been spending a lot of time together lately, haven't they?" Randy continued in the same serious tone.

"I guess so," I said, shrugging.

"Come on, Katie," Sabs cut in quickly. "You've got to help me with our locker. I'm afraid to open it. All my stuff is going to come crashing down and bury me in an avalanche."

Sabs and I share a locker. I usually keep my half really organized, but neatness is not one of Sabs's strong points. It really does take two people to keep from being buried by her books when you open the door.

Anyway, before I could say anything more to Randy, Sabs was pulling me off to our locker. It looked like I would have to wait until tomorrow to ask Randy what she thought was so strange about my family going to dinner with Michel and Jean-Paul Beauvais.

Chapter Two

"Are you ready yet, Katie?" my mom called from downstairs.

"Just a sec, Mom!" I called back as I searched in my closet for my other black flat.

"The reservation's at seven, Katie," my mom continued. "We're going to be late."

"When is Emily meeting us over there?" I asked over my shoulder, still looking for my shoe. Emily is on the high school yearbook staff, and she had a late meeting that night.

"She's probably there already," my mother replied. Her voice sounded a lot closer now, and I saw that she had come up the stairs and was standing in the doorway to my room, waiting for me. "Let's go. I don't want to keep Jean-Paul waiting."

Finally I found the shoe and stood up. Slipping my foot in, I took one last glimpse in the mirror. I had to admit that I really liked my new dress. It was teal green and had a dropped waist. I had French-braided my hair and tied a teal bow at the end. I still couldn't figure out why my mom had gotten me a new dress to wear out to dinner in the middle of the week, though. We hardly ever went out on school nights, much less to a fancy restaurant we had to get all dressed up for. My mom had even lent me a string of pearls that my dad had given her, to wear with my new dress.

"You look very nice," Mom complimented me, coming up behind me. I glanced at her reflection behind me.

"You do, too, Mom!" I exclaimed. She did look great. Her simple black dress was very elegant, and her blond hair had been highlighted and styled the day before. She was also wearing black pumps and carrying a small black handbag with a gold clasp. I almost couldn't believe that this glamorous person was my mother.

"Thanks, honey," she said, smiling anxiously at me. Then she took my hand and pulled me out of my room, saying again, "Let's get going." She seemed really keyed up about something. I hadn't seen her in this much of a tizzy since she had first started dating Jean-Paul.

"So, how do you like Jean-Paul?" my mom asked as soon as we got in the car. I mean, we weren't even out of the driveway yet. What was she so tense about?

"Mom, you know I like him," I replied.

"I just want you to *really* like him," she added. "I think he's wonderful, and I hope that both of you girls feel the same way."

I turned in my seat to look at my mom. Wonderful? I mean, I liked Jean-Paul and all, but I really didn't know him well enough to think he was wonderful — at least, not in the way I thought my dad was wonderful. "I think he's nice," I said truthfully.

"Oh, Mom, I wanted to ask you something," I added, changing the subject. All this talk about Jean-Paul was making me nervous for some reason.

"Yes, dear?" my mom asked, sounding distracted.

"We're having a sixties dance at school," I told her. "Did you save any clothes from those days? Do we have anything up in the attic?"

My mom waved a hand in the air and said, "There's bound to be something up there. You know what a pack rat your father was."

She turned to give me a curious look. "You really want clothes from the sixties?" she asked dubiously.

"Definitely, Mom," I answered. "Everyone has to come in costume."

Mom laughed, exclaiming, "Costume! You know, Katie, I used to wear those clothes when I was a little older than Emily. And now they're costumes. I feel old."

"You're not old, Mom!" I protested. "It's just that the sixties were a long time ago."

Mom groaned. "That proves it, I *am* old!"

I really hadn't meant it that way, even though the sixties *were* a long time ago. "Sorry," I mumbled.

"That's okay, dear," Mom told me lightly. "Actually, I don't feel old at all. Especially not tonight."

I wanted to ask her what she meant by that, but I didn't have a chance because my mom turned on the radio and started singing along. She kept it up until we pulled into the parking lot of Chez Pierre. Chez Pierre is probably the most expensive restaurant in Acorn Falls. I had never been there before — my mother had never been able to afford to take us there. But

Jean-Paul is pretty well off. At first I thought it must be cool for Michel not to have to worry about money. But actually I don't think it's all that great. His dad isn't home much because he's always traveling on business. Jean-Paul even missed one of our big hockey playoff games, and I'm pretty sure Michel was upset about it. I know we don't have a lot of money, but it's never bothered me. I mean, at least Mom made it to all my home games.

"Oh, Emily's not here yet," Mom said in a disappointed voice as the maître d' showed us to a table where Michel and his dad were already seated.

"Eileen!" Jean-Paul exclaimed, standing up as we got to the table. He leaned over and gave my mom a quick kiss, then took both of her hands and led her to a chair. "You look *merveilleuse*."

Mom blushed and said, "Thank you."

"Katie, *comment ça va*?" he said, turning to me. "How are you?"

"*Bien*," I replied, giving Jean-Paul a kiss on the cheek. "*Et vous*?"

"*Tr`es bien*," he answered, smiling at my mother.

"K.C., you look very nice," Michel said as we all sat down.

"*Merci*," I replied. "So do you." He was wearing a navy blue suit and a tie. I had never seen him in a suit before — not even at the hockey awards dinner.

"I wonder where Emily is?" my mother asked nervously after Jean-Paul had ordered a bottle of champagne and five glasses. I had never had champagne before, but Michel's dad said the situation warranted it. *What situation?* Why was tonight's dinner such a big deal?

"I'm sure she'll get here soon," I replied calmly, wondering what the rush was. Emily is usually extremely punctual, and my mother knows that. It wasn't like Mom to worry this way.

"I know, I know," my mother said, taking a deep breath. "I'm just excited."

"*Oui*," Jean-Paul agreed. "*Moi aussi*. Me, too." When I glanced at Michel, I noticed that he looked as confused as I felt. That made me feel a little better. Finally he threw his hands up in the air.

"Aaayy!" Michel exclaimed. "What is going on?" he asked his father. "You have been acting

15

strangely all week."

"We'd better wait until Emily gets here," my mother said, answering for Jean-Paul.

"Wait for what?" I asked, but my mom just patted my arm and told me to be patient. I was starting to get a funny feeling in my stomach. I realized that whatever was going on must have to do with more than just food.

After five long, uncomfortable minutes, Emily breezed in. As usual, she looked perfect in a pale pink linen dress. The sick thing was that she had worn it to school all that day, and hadn't gotten a wrinkle in it or a spot on it. My sister was born perfect, that's all there is to it. I don't even try to compete with her. My friends think that we look a lot alike — Emily has blond hair and blue eyes, too. But I think they're crazy.

"Emily, where were you?" Mom demanded as soon as my sister sat down.

"Mother," Emily protested. "I told you I was going to be late. I had a yearbook meeting."

"But I told you to meet us here at seven," Mom replied. "It's nearly ten after."

"Eileen," Jean-Paul cut in. "It is all right. She is here now."

"*Mon Dieu!*" Michel exclaimed. "Are you

going to let us in on the big secret now? What is going on?"

Emily looked at me in confusion. "What big secret?" she asked. I shrugged, feeling anxious. I don't like secrets. They always mean that someone is left out.

Jean-Paul gave my mother a big smile. "First, let me pour the champagne," he said, reaching for the bottle. Everyone was quiet as he poured. I held my breath until he put the bottle down and raised his glass. "I'd like to propose a toast to Eileen," he said, looking into my mother's eyes. I shifted uncomfortably in my seat. What did they need us here for if they were just going to toast each other? Why wouldn't the nervous feeling in the pit of my stomach go away?"

". . . who said yes when I asked her to be my wife," Jean-Paul concluded, turning to Michel, Emily, and me with a huge grin.

"Mon Dieu!" Michel exclaimed again. "That is wonderful. I am very excited." I barely heard him. I felt as if someone had pulled the chair out from under me and I was going to hit the hard floor any second. I couldn't believe it. My mother was getting married! This couldn't be

happening. It wasn't real. It had to be a dream.

"K.C., you are going to be my sister!" Michel went on, grinning. "This is very great!"

I stared at him blankly. I had never had a brother. And I didn't know if I wanted one, either.

"And, Eileen," Michel continued, looking at my mother. "You are going to be my new mother. It will be nice to have one. You know, I never really knew my real mother."

Mother? She was *my* mother, and I wasn't going to share her. No way!

I looked at Jean-Paul. I certainly hoped that he didn't think he was going to be my new father. I had already had a father, one that I had really loved. I still missed him, and I didn't want a new one.

"Well, Katie? Emily?" Mom asked, looking at us with a big smile on her face. For the first time I looked at Emily. Her face was really stiff.

It looked as if someone had carved it from a block of ice or something. "That's great, Mom," she said in a very flat voice. "Really great. Congratulations, Jean-Paul." Then she picked up her menu and opened it.

My mom's face fell. "Katie?" she asked hesitantly. I didn't think this was going quite the way she planned it. But how did she expect us to react? Dad had only died three years ago. We didn't even know Jean-Paul very well.

"Congratulations," I said softly, trying to smile. I didn't want to hurt my mother's feelings or anything, but I couldn't say anything more. I knew if I did I would start crying. I didn't feel like celebrating at all. What I really felt like doing was standing up and screaming. How could my mother do this?

Chapter Three

For the next few days I felt as if my whole world had fallen apart. I really didn't feel like talking about the wedding at all. I mean, I'd told my friends all about my mother and Jean-Paul the very next morning. But after that I really avoided the subject. I'm not sure why. Maybe I thought that if I didn't think or talk about it, the wedding would just not happen.

I was still in a daze by Friday night, when Allison, Randy, and I went over to Sabs's house for a sleep-over. But I was trying to be cheerful for my friends' sake. The wedding wasn't their problem.

"Check out these pants!" Sabs exclaimed, holding up a pair of red, white, and blue bell-bottoms.

"Perfect!" Randy pronounced. "Try them on." We were all up in Sabs's attic bedroom, going through five boxes of clothes that her

20

mother had found in the basement. It looked as if Mrs. Wells had saved everything she'd ever worn in her life.

Sabs quickly pulled on the bell-bottoms. "They don't fit!" she wailed, trying to tug them higher. "They don't go up far enough. They don't even come to my waist!"

"Let me see," said Randy, and Sabs turned so we could all get a look. The pants were low on her hips and fit kind of snugly, until they got to her knees. Then they flared out in a major way.

I could understand why they were called bell-bottoms. "That's the way they are supposed to be," Randy announced. "They're hip-huggers."

"No way!" Sabs exclaimed. "This is right? They feel really weird. How do they look?"

Allison glanced over at me and started giggling. Even though I wasn't in a great mood, I couldn't help laughing, too.

"What's so funny?" Sabs asked, walking over to her full-length mirror. Then she caught a glimpse of herself, and her mouth fell open.

"How could my mom have worn these?" Sabs asked, totally cracking up. "These are too weird."

She started to unzip the bell-bottoms, but Randy said, "No! You've got to wear them, Sabs. They're perfect for this dance."

Sabs giggled as she stared at her reflection again.

"What shirt are you going to wear with them?" Allison asked, looking up from the box she was rummaging in.

A moment later I pulled out a purple ribbed sleeveless turtleneck.

"How about this one?" I offered.

"It doesn't match," Sabs said, taking the turtleneck and holding it up next to the red, white, and blue pants.

"So?" Randy returned with a laugh. "It's probably better that way. People used to wear totally outrageous color combinations in the sixties."

Sabs pulled the turtleneck on, tucked it into the bell-bottoms, and went back to the mirror. "This is definitely a happening outfit, guys."

"Here are some shoes," said Al, handing Sabs a pair of black platform sandals. "I think these will look perfect."

"Gosh!" Sabs exclaimed, looking questioningly at the shoes. "Do you really think I should wear these?" She stepped into them, then bent to fasten the buckles.

"I can't believe it, I'm two whole inches taller. I *have* to wear them — all the time!" Everyone burst out laughing. Sabs *is* kind of on the short side.

"Sabs, you're going to be the best-dressed person there," Randy said after we had all stopped laughing. "Hey, do you mind if I borrow this?" She held up a silver belt made out of a bunch of overlapping circles.

"Sure," said Sabs, nodding. "Are you going to wear it with that minidress you were telling us about?"

Randy shook her head. "I've got a better outfit now," she said. "It's a cat suit my mom had from the sixties. The belt will look great with it."

"What are you two wearing?" Sabs asked, turning to Allison and me. "Did you find anything in these boxes that you want to borrow?"

Mrs. Wells had some great old clothes, but I thought it would be nice to wear something of my mom's to the dance, that is, if she'd saved anything from the sixties.

"I'm going to check out my attic first," I said,

promising myself to go through the stuff up there as soon as possible. "I'll let you know, okay? At least I know I have a couple of places to look."

"How about you, Al?" Randy asked, without looking up from the box she was digging through. "Wow, this is excellent!" Randy grinned as she pulled out a golden-yellow, long-sleeved, crushed-velvet minidress. "This is major! You have to wear it, Al!" I could tell by the look on Al's face that she wasn't sure the dress was a great idea. It did look awfully short and kind of flashy. And Al is a pretty shy person.

"I don't think so," she said at first. "It just isn't me, guys."

"Try it on," Randy urged, handing the dress to Al.

"Well . . ." Al began.

"Al, you have to!" Sabs broke in excitedly, cutting her off. "It's fab!"

Five minutes later, Al had definitely become a sixties go-go girl. I have to say, the dress looked fantastic on her. I guess being five feet seven helped. Randy found a maroon velvet hat for Al to wear. But the best part of the outfit was the white vinyl zip-up go-go boots that Sabs found.

"This is so wild-looking," Allison said when Randy and Sabs let her look in the mirror.

"But you look perfect," Sabs told her, changing out of her sixties stuff and into her pink polka-dotted pajamas. "You have to wear it."

With a final look at her reflection in the mirror, Al said, "Well, just let me think about it a few days, Sabs. I'm just not quite sure. Besides, the dance isn't for another month, anyway." Then she gave Sabs a big smile.

"Well, remember, it looks *perfectly sixties* on you," Sabs said with satisfaction in her voice.

Al cracked up and started changing her clothes as well.

"All right!" Randy announced after we were all wearing our pajamas. "It's time for the feature flick!"

"Oh, no!" Sabs exclaimed. "I forgot you were renting the movie. Don't tell me it's another horror movie."

Randy just grinned, so I knew it definitely was. Randy loves horror movies. She's probably seen every one that's ever been made.

"What did you rent, Randy?" I asked with a sigh.

"It's a classic," Randy said, pulling a video-tape cassette out of her knapsack. "You guys are going to love it."

"We're in major trouble!" Sabs exclaimed. "I better bring an extra pillow down to hug." Sabs gets really scared watching horror movies, though I don't know why. Most of them are obviously fake. It's not like any of that stuff could ever really happen or anything.

"What's it called?" I asked again.

"Well, I was going to get *Slumber Party Massacre II*," Randy replied. "But then I remembered how much you guys hated the first one." We all shook our heads in agreement.

"That was gross!" Sabs said, her face wrinkled up in distaste.

"I'm glad you didn't get the sequel," Al added.

"Sooo, I got . . . *The Blob* . . . instead," Randy continued.

"The original?" Allison asked, sounding excited. I had to admit that I didn't even know there was an original and a remake. It figures Al would. She's like a walking Library of Congress. Sometimes I think that every fact known to man must be registered somewhere in her brain. It's pretty incredible.

"The remake," said Randy continuing. "Don't worry, Sabs. You'll like it."

"Seriously?" Sabs asked, brightening a little. She headed for the door and started clattering down the stairs. "Let's get down to the living room before Sam and his friends decide to play Nintendo or watch TV or something."

Sam is Sabs's twin brother, who is older than her by all of four minutes. He and his best friends, Nick Robbins and Jason McKee, spend a lot of time playing video games. Luckily, we didn't see the guys anywhere, so we got the VCR all set up. Then we all trooped out to the kitchen and sat around the kitchen table while Sabs found a bag of microwave popcorn and stuck it in the microwave oven.

"Katie, I still can't believe your mom's getting married," Sabs said as she set the timer. "You must be totally excited! I mean, Mr. Beauvais is really rich, isn't he? Your mom won't have to work anymore if she doesn't want to, or anything."

"She likes to work," I said softly. Suddenly the whole wedding thing came rushing back into my mind.

I should have known that my friends would ask about it sooner or later. I guess I could understand why Sabs would think I'd be excited — she knew I'd never been to a wedding before, much less my own mom's. But I really didn't want to talk about it. I mean, Sabs is my best friend in the world, but I just didn't think she would understand why I wasn't happy, too. Especially since she was so psyched about it.

"You know, I've always wanted to be in a wedding party," Sabs continued in this dreamy voice. "What color do you think your bridesmaid dress is going to be? Do you know where they're getting married? Are we invited?"

"Of course you are," I said quickly. Actually, I hadn't talked to my mom about that yet. But suddenly I knew my best friends had to be invited. I didn't think I could get through that day if they weren't with me.

"So, what colors are you wearing?" Sabs asked again.

"Who's going to be the maid of honor?" Al wanted to know. It didn't look like there was any way I could get out of answering their questions. So I took a deep breath and plunged in.

"The matron of honor, you mean," I corrected Al. "My Aunt Elizabeth. She's my mom's sister, but since she's already married she's called a matron of honor instead of a maid. Emily and I are the only bridesmaids, but I have no idea what colors we're wearing yet. I don't think my mom's picked them out. They're getting married at the Congregational Church, and the reception is at the Acorn Falls Country Club." I felt as if I was reciting a grocery list or something. I tried to sound excited, but my voice came out sounding flat. Luckily, my friends didn't seem to notice.

"That place is beautiful!" Sabs exclaimed. "I've never been there, but I hear that there are chandeliers in the bathrooms. Oh, Katie, aren't you excited? It's going to be great. I can't wait, and it's not even my mother."

"Sure," I said tonelessly.

"And Michel is going to be your new brother," Sabs said, bouncing excitedly around the kitchen. "That's wild. I'd love to have him for a brother. He's so nice and cute and everything."

Just then the bell sounded on the microwave, so I didn't have to reply. Jumping up from the table, I filled the bowl with popcorn. Anything to keep from continuing this conversation.

"Come on, guys. We don't want to keep *The Blob* waiting," I said. We had just settled on the sofa when I realized we had forgotten to bring in napkins and cola. I jumped up to get them.

"I'll come with you," Randy offered, following me back into the kitchen. I didn't say anything as I pulled the soda pop bottle out of the refrigerator and dug around in the narrow cabinet next to the oven for a tray.

"You're not really happy about this wedding thing, are you?" Randy asked quietly as she put four glasses on the tray. I could feel tears rising to my eyes, so I quickly opened the freezer door, sticking my head way in while I reached for the ice tray.

"What are you talking about?" I asked.

Randy looked at me, and said quietly, "I know I would hate it if my mom got remarried, especially after just getting divorced from my dad last year. And you don't exactly seem thrilled about this situation."

Suddenly I felt as if I had to tell someone how I really felt or I would burst. I had been keeping it all in for two days. Emily wouldn't even talk about it. In fact, she was hardly ever home. She just ate and slept there and wouldn't say much to anybody. I knew she was really upset, but it hurt me that she wouldn't even talk to me about it. After all, I was upset, too.

Blinking back my tears, I turned to look at Randy. "My dad's only been dead for three years," I said, throwing ice cubes in the glasses. "How could my mom get married again?" Randy shrugged and gave me a sympathetic look. "And to Jean-Paul!" I continued angrily.

"Wait a minute," Randy said, sounding confused. "I thought you liked him."

"I did — I mean, I do," I said. "I just didn't think he'd ask my mom to marry him. And I can't believe she said yes."

I wasn't sure if what I said even made sense. I just knew it was how I felt. I was relieved when Randy nodded. She really seemed to understand everything I was talking about. "I mean, she didn't even talk to Emily and me first," I added.

Randy laughed at that. "What was she going to say — 'Girls, Jean-Paul wants to get married. What should I do? Should I say yes, play a little hard to get, or dump him? Maybe I should hold out for a bigger diamond.'"

31

I couldn't imagine Mom doing that at all. I smiled a little at the thought.

"Aha!" Randy exclaimed. "See, it's not the end of the world. You had a little smile there."

I guessed she had a point. But still . . . "It's just that he's so different from my dad," I told her. "How could my mom even think of marrying him?"

"Maybe that's the point," Randy said, after a moment. "Maybe it's good that he's not somebody your mom can compare to your dad. You wouldn't want him to be a clone or anything."

I shook my head vigorously. "No way!" I leaned my elbows on the Wellses' counter. "I guess you're right," I admitted. "I want my mom to be happy. But it's all so sudden. I mean, I feel as if they just met."

"It sounds as if you're a little shell-shocked," Randy said. "It's probably just happening so fast that you haven't had enough time to get a grip on it."

That made sense. I was really grateful that Randy understood what I was feeling. It was funny, I was usually the most logical one of my friends. But obviously this was one thing I couldn't think about objectively.

"Listen, we'd better get back to the flick," said Randy. "Sabs and Al are going to wonder what happened." I nodded. "Uh, Ran . . ." I began and then trailed off. Randy picked up the tray and paused.

"What?"

"Don't tell Sabs and Al about this, okay?" I said quietly. "Sabs is so excited about this wedding and all, I just don't want to go into why I'm not."

Giving me a quick nod, Randy said, "Not a problem."

"Besides, maybe I'll get more excited by the time the wedding happens, so everyone will have gotten worried for nothing," I concluded. Randy and I walked back into the living room and settled on the sofa. I sat back as Randy popped the tape in, but I couldn't concentrate on the movie. I thought about what Randy and I had talked about in the kitchen. Maybe I just needed a little time to get a grip on things, like she'd said. I hoped she was right.

Chapter Four

"Katie!" I heard Mom call out while I was in the shower. Sighing to myself, I turned off the water, grabbed a towel, and stepped out of the tub. For the past three weeks, my mother had kept me busy just about every second I wasn't at school or doing my homework. She was going crazy planning the wedding. I had intended to take Randy's advice and just let myself get used to the whole wedding thing. But I had been so busy that I hadn't had time to get used to anything.

After drying off, I wrapped my bathrobe around me and walked out of the bathroom.

"Oh, there you are, Katie," Mom said as she came out of my bedroom. "I was just looking for you. I need you to pick up the napkins and then stop by the florist on the way back to drop off this check," she said, handing me an envelope. I stifled a bubble of disappointment. I had been planning to head over to the mall today with my friends, but I could see that was out of the question now. Mom had me booked for another Saturday.

Boy, would I be relieved when this wedding was over. Just one more week to go.

"I don't know how I ever did this the first time," my mom added with a sigh. "It's so much work." Then she snapped her fingers and said, "Oh, Grandma and Grandpa Ryan called me this morning. They'll need to stay here, too."

Great, I thought. We now had seven people staying with us: Aunt Elizabeth and Uncle Ted, Mom's cousin Jessie and her husband, Mike, my Great-uncle Max, plus Grandma and Grandpa Ryan. I felt as if we were running a hotel, besides which I had no idea where in the world we were going to put them all.

"I hate to rush you, Katie," Mom continued, already turning and walking down the stairs. "But I really need to get those napkins so I can get them over to the caterer by eleven. And I've got an appointment with the photographer in half an hour."

I nodded and headed into my room to get

dressed. A hot breakfast was out of the question, I could see. My mom used to make Emily and me pancakes every Saturday and Sunday morning before she got engaged. Now Emily was never even home anymore, and I was lucky to get a bowl of cold cereal. I dressed in jeans and a peach cable-knit cotton sweater, then headed downstairs. As I walked into the kitchen, I heard my mom's car pull out of the driveway. I felt as if I never saw her anymore. What with her work and this wedding, she was constantly on the go. I had wanted to talk to her about Jean-Paul and Dad and everything — I thought maybe she could help me straighten everything out in my mind. But there never seemed to be any time.

I spotted a note propped up in front of the sugar bowl on the kitchen table. Walking over to the table, I picked up the note and read it:

Katie,

Don't forget about your 11:30 appointment at Betty Sue's Bridal Shop for your last fitting. If you see your sister, please remind her, too.

Love,
Mom

Who knew if I would see Emily? She was spending all her time with her boyfriend, Reed, and her best friend, Sarah. Meanwhile, I was getting stuck with all the work. All I could do was write her name on Mom's note, too, so she would read it if she came home.

Then I quickly ate a bowl of cereal, called Sabs to say I couldn't go to the mall, grabbed my jacket, and headed outside. The napkins were being printed at Ecco's Stationery on Main Street. It wasn't that far a walk, and it felt good to be outside on such a beautiful morning. Taking a deep breath, I tried to put the wedding out of my mind. I just wanted to enjoy the day.

"K.C.!" I heard someone call out behind me as I rounded the corner at the end of my block. I turned around and saw Scottie Silver running down the sidewalk toward me. He was wearing a T-shirt, running shorts, and sneakers. Obviously he was taking Coach Budd's conditioning meeting seriously.

"Hi, Scottie," I greeted him when he caught up with me. "Don't tell me you're in training already?" Scottie slowed to a walk and fell into step beside me.

"Yup. I thought I'd get a regular running

routine in the off-season," he said. "High school hockey is probably going to be much tougher than junior high. The Bradley High center is going to be a senior next year, and he's really huge. Of course, I'd never start as a freshman, but I want some playing time."

I couldn't believe it. The great Scottie Silver was worried about making the team! He's usually so incredibly confident about his abilities.

"I'm sure you have nothing to worry about," I told him. "You're a really good hockey player."

"Thanks, K.C. Well, I guess we'll see," Scottie said, shrugging. We walked quietly for a while, and it suddenly started to hit me that Scottie wouldn't be playing on my team next year. "I'm really going to miss you beating me up on the ice next year," I said quietly, looking down at my sneakers. I couldn't believe how much things were changing. I wished we'd have exactly the same team as we'd had this past season. It had been great.

"It'll be weird," Scottie admitted. When I looked up, I saw that his bright blue eyes were fixed on mine.

"But you know, K.C., you'll be playing to the

left of me again in no time at all."

I wasn't so sure about that. "I heard they were thinking about starting a girls' hockey team at the high school," I told him.

"Seriously?" Scottie asked, looking shocked. "But you have to play on our team. You don't really want to play with a bunch of girls, do you?"

I laughed. "Scottie, I *am* a girl."

Scottie's face turned bright red, and he said, "I know, I know. It's just that . . . " His voice trailed off, and neither of us said anything for a moment. Then Scottie sort of cleared his throat and said, "I've got some good news for you, K.C."

"I could sure use it," I told him.

Scottie gave me this really big smile. "I had a long talk with the coach last night about next year's team," he explained. "And he's worried about keeping the team tight and everything."

"Oh. You mean, because so many guys are graduating?" I asked, frowning. That could be a problem.

"Yeah," Scottie replied. "He needs a new captain" — he paused for a second, and his smile grew even wider — "and it looks like it's going to be you."

My mouth fell open, and I just stared at Scottie. "Me?" I asked, finally finding my voice. "I'm going to be captain next year? I don't believe it! What about Michel? He's a great player." Michel's the best hockey player our school has ever seen. He's not the highest scorer, but that's only because he joined the team near the end of the season. I've never seen skating like his before in my life — except on my dad's semipro team. I guess it's because he's from Canada. They start kids really young up there. I think they're born with hockey skates on.

"Michel's good, there's no doubt about it," Scottie said. "But, K.C., the coach knows you're a real team player, and he thinks you're a great example to everyone. You work hard, and you play all out every game."

It made me feel great to be hearing all this. I mean, I did work hard for the team. But it still didn't seem fair to Michel.

"So does Michel," I protested.

"Well, he's not going to be captain," Scottie said matter-of-factly. "You are."

I still couldn't believe it! I couldn't wait to

tell my mom. I kind of wondered how Jean-Paul would react to the news. After all, his own son wasn't going to be captain. I was. Suddenly I wished my dad could be there. He had taught me how to skate when I was four, and I knew he'd be really proud of me right now if he was still alive.

"I'd better get back to my run," Scottie said, breaking into my thoughts. He ran his hand through his curly blond hair. "I've got three more miles to go."

"Okay," I said distractedly. "See you later, Scottie."

Scottie started running down the sidewalk. When he was about ten yards in front of me, he stopped and spun around. "Oh, K.C.!" he called out. "Are you going to the sixties dance next Saturday?"

I gasped. Next Saturday was the day of Mom's wedding! But then I calmed down when I remembered that my mom had said the reception would be over by late afternoon. The dance didn't start until seven-thirty.

"Yes!" I called back, answering Scottie.

"Great!" he yelled with a wave. "I'll definitely see you there! Save me a dance."

I grinned at Scottie's retreating back. The day was really starting to look up. I was going to be captain of next year's hockey team, and Scottie Silver wanted me to save him a dance!

An hour later, I walked back into the house. I could hear my mother in the kitchen pulling the dishes out of the dishwasher.

"Hi, Mom," I said, dropping the bag with the napkins in it on the table. I couldn't wait to tell her my good news. "You're not going to believe this —" I began.

"Hello, dear," my mom said. "Oh, are those the napkins? Great." She walked over, opened the bag, and pulled out the napkins. "Oh, no!" she exclaimed. "These aren't the right color. These are lilac. I wanted cream with blue lettering. Didn't you check them at Ecco's?" I had. The names were spelled right, and the date was correct. That was all I'd looked for, since I didn't know what color my mom had ordered anyway.

"Now I'm going to have to go all the way back over there to get this straightened out," Mom said, frowning as she put the napkins back in the bag. "And I can't bring the caterers the napkins, so I'm going to have to make another appointment. I hope Ecco's can get new ones printed in time."

She closed up the bag, picked it up with a sigh, and walked out of the kitchen, talking to herself.

"I'm going to be captain of the hockey team next year," I whispered to the empty kitchen. Suddenly I didn't feel very excited anymore. I was glad no one was there to see the tears that started running down my cheeks.

Chapter Five

Sabs calls Katie.

KATIE: Campbell residence, Katie speak-
            ing.
SABS: Katie? This is Sabs. How're you
            doing?
KATIE: Hi, Sabs. I'm okay.
SABS: What's the matter, Katie? You
            sound kind of down. The wed-
            ding's only a week away. Aren't
            you getting excited? When are all
            your relatives coming?
KATIE: Oh, I'm all right. Everyone's
            arriving next Friday. It's probably
            going to get really crazy around
            here.
SABS: But it will probably be good
            crazy, right? I mean, you haven't
            seen them in a while, right?
KATIE: Not since we went to stay with
            them in Minneapolis last

	Christmas. I guess it will be fun.
SABS:	I'm sorry you couldn't come with us to the mall today. I found a really cool dress to wear to the wedding. It's got spaghetti straps and everything. Did you get those napkins and do everything you had to do?
KATIE:	I got them, but they were the wrong color, so they have to be reprinted. Mom nearly had a fit. Listen, I better get off, Sabs. I have to finish making out place cards.
SABS:	Place cards?
KATIE:	For the reception. There's one with each person's name on it, so everyone knows where to sit. I'm writing the names on the cards.
SABS:	Cool! Well, I'll see you at school on Monday, okay? Oh, and thank your mom for the great invitation. It was exciting to get one. I don't think I have ever gotten anything so elegant in the mail in my whole life.

KATIE:	They are nice. I addressed most of them, Sabs.
SABS:	Wow. That must have been a lot of work. Anyway, I'll see you tomorrow, Katie.
KATIE:	Okay, bye.
SABS:	Bye.

Sabs calls Randy.

RANDY:	Talk to me.
SABS:	Randy. Hi, it's me. Listen, I just talked to Katie, and she's not sounding very happy at all. Do you know what's bothering her?
RANDY:	Well . . .
SABS:	You do know. Randy, you have to tell me!
RANDY:	I can't, Sabs. Katie swore me to secrecy.
SABS:	It must be really serious if she's not even talking to me about it. What could she be so upset about? I mean, her mom's wedding is really exciting and everything.

(There is a long pause.)

SABS:	Don't tell me that's what's bothering her? You mean she's not happy about the wedding? I don't believe it!

(There is another silence.)

SABS:	Randy, is that it? You have to tell me so we can do something to help!
RANDY:	Well . . . Remember you had that sleep-over a couple of days after her mother first got engaged?
SABS:	Yeah?
RANDY:	Well, Katie told me that she wasn't totally thrilled about her mom getting married again. She didn't want to say anything because you were really psyched about the wedding, and she didn't want to bring you down.
SABS:	But we're her best friends! If she's upset, I definitely want to know about it and try to help. Does Al know?
RANDY:	No. The only reason Katie even

	said anything to me is because I guessed. Besides, she figured she'd get used to the whole idea, so there wouldn't be a problem anymore.
SABS:	It doesn't sound like she is used to it. Maybe I should call her back. I know! I'll call Al first. She'll know exactly what to say.
RANDY:	Good idea. Look, Sabs, my mom needs to use the phone. I'd better get off.
SABS:	Okay. See you tomorrow.
RANDY:	*Ciao.* Oh, let me know what happens with Al and Katie?
SABS:	Sure. Bye.

Sabs calls Allison. Charlie picks up the phone, says "Hi," then drops the phone. About a minute later, Allison picks up the receiver.

ALLISON:	Hello, is anyone there?
SABS:	Al? Thank goodness you're there!
ALLISON:	Sabs! How long have you been on the phone?
SABS:	Absolutely forever. Listen, Al. You've got to help me. We've got

	to talk to Katie. She's really upset about the wedding.
ALLISON:	I figured she was.
SABS:	You know, too?
ALLISON:	Well, I just guessed. She hasn't seemed too happy lately.
SABS:	I can't believe I was so dense I didn't even notice. I feel awful.
ALLISON:	So, what do you want to do?
SABS:	I want to call her and tell her she can talk to any of us if she wants to.
ALLISON:	That sounds like a really good idea.
SABS:	Do you think that's enough?
ALLISON:	It's a start. Maybe we can think of something nice to do before the wedding.
SABS:	That's a great idea! Maybe we can help her get ready or something. That way we could cheer her up before the ceremony. Do you think she'd like that?
ALLISON:	Why don't you call her and ask? Oh — did you hear? Billy told me that Scottie told him that Katie is

	going to be named captain of the ice hockey team next year.
SABS:	Seriously? That's fantastic! Why didn't she tell us that?
ALLISON:	Maybe she didn't feel as if it was important, with her mother getting married and everything.
SABS:	What do you mean?
ALLISON:	I think weddings take a lot of planning. You know how busy Katie's been. She hasn't been able to do anything with us for practically the last month. I think it's kind of taken over her life.
SABS:	Seriously. Katie just told me that her mother is getting crazy over napkins. Can you believe it?
ALLISON:	I think there are a lot of details like that to take care of.
SABS:	Well, I guess I should call her back now.
ALLISON:	Okay. Good luck.
SABS:	Thanks. Bye, Al.
ALLISON:	Good-bye.

Sabs calls Katie back.

KATIE: Hello, Katie speaking.

SABS: Hi, Katie. It's me again.

KATIE: Hi, Sabs.

SABS: Congratulations!

KATIE: What are you talking about? I'm not getting married.

SABS: I just heard you're going to be captain of the team next year! That's fantastic!

KATIE: Oh, thanks. I almost forgot all about that.

SABS: Forgot? How could you? It's so exciting. I can't believe you're going to be captain.

KATIE: I guess it is exciting. I'm still kind of in shock about it.

SABS: Your mom must be really proud of you. She was really getting into hockey by the end of the season, right?

(There is a short pause.)

KATIE: She doesn't know.

SABS: You didn't tell her? Why not?

KATIE: Well, I tried. But then she got all upset about those napkins I was

	telling you about.
SABS:	Katie, are you all right? You don't sound very happy.
KATIE:	I'm okay.
SABS:	Come on, Katie. This is me, Sabs.
KATIE:	Well . . .
SABS:	What? Come on, out with it.
KATIE:	I guess I'm just not used to the idea that my mom's getting married. I thought I would be by now. But I'm not, and the wedding's next week.
SABS:	I'm sure it'll be okay.
KATIE:	Probably. It's just that my mom's been so busy I haven't even been able to talk to her. Sometimes it's like I'm not even in the room. And Emily's never here. Things are really changing, and I don't know if I like all of the changes.
SABS:	Things always change. I mean, think about how boring everything would be if nothing ever changed.
KATIE:	I guess. But everything's happening too fast. I'm sorry, Sabs. I

know you're really excited about the wedding. We can talk about something else if you want.

SABS: Katie, if this is bothering you, I definitely want to talk about it — if you do, that is. That's what friends are for.

KATIE: Thanks.

SABS: I was thinking, do you think it would be cool if Randy, Al, and I came over to your house before the wedding? We could help you get ready and everything. I think it would be fun — if you think it's a good idea, that is.

KATIE: That would be great. It would really mean a lot to me to have you guys around. I'm not sure my mom will let me, though. There are going to be tons of people here already.

SABS: Well, ask her about it, okay? Not to change the subject, but to change the subject, did you find an outfit for the sixties dance yet?

KATIE: Oh, I forgot all about it! I'll have

to look at the stuff in our attic
sometime this week.

SABS: Don't worry if you don't find
            anything. There's still tons of stuff
            in those boxes of my mom's. I'm
            really happy you're going to be
            staying with me while your mom
            and Mr. Beauvais are on their
            honeymoon. You're coming to my
            house after the reception, right?

KATIE: Right. My mom and Jean-Paul are
            leaving for France right away.
            And my relatives are all leaving
            after the reception, too. It should
            be over by four or five o'clock.

SABS: I can't wait. We're going to be
            staying together for two weeks!
            You know that Michel is staying
            with us, too, right? In Sam and
            Mark's room.

KATIE: He is? I didn't know that. I guess
            Mom forgot to tell me. She's been
            kind of distracted lately.

SABS: It'll be great!

KATIE: Listen, Sabs, thanks for calling.
            You know, I feel a little better. I'm

	going to go find my mom and see if she's got a minute now.
SABS:	Good luck. I hope she says yes about us coming over. And don't forget to tell her about making captain, okay?
KATIE:	All right. So, I'll see you guys on Monday. And, Sabs?
SABS:	Yeah?
KATIE:	Thanks. Thanks a lot.
SABS:	No problem. Bye, Katie!
KATIE:	Bye.

Chapter Six

As soon as I got off the phone, I went searching for my mom. I found her at the kitchen table, finishing up the place cards I had started on.

"Mom?" I asked, sitting down next to her. My mom finished writing a name out on one of the cards and put it on top of the stack of finished ones.

"What is it, Katie?" she asked, starting on a new card without looking up.

"Do you think it would be okay if Sabs, Al, and Randy come over next Saturday before the wedding to help me get ready?" I asked.

Glancing distractedly over at me, my mom said, "But, Katie, we're already going to be tripping all over one another, with Grandma and Grandpa and everyone staying here and the photographer taking pictures. I really don't think having three more people in the house is a good idea. They'll just get in the way." Then she turned back to the place cards. I bit my lip and looked down at my lap.

"Oh. I guess you're right," I said quietly. Out of the corner of my eye, I saw my mom shoot me a look. I didn't look back because I was afraid I would start crying.

"On second thought," she said after a pause, "maybe you could use some extra help, honey. Go ahead and invite your friends if you want to."

"Really? Thanks, Mom!" I said, jumping up and giving her a hug. If my friends were going to be with me, this whole wedding thing couldn't be all bad. I was about to run and call back Sabs, when I remembered my promise to tell Mom about being captain of the hockey team next year.

"Katie, that's terrific!" my mom exclaimed when I told her. "I'm so proud of you. You certainly deserve it, after the way you played so well all season."

Suddenly I found myself smiling. "Do you want me to finish up the cards, Mom?" I asked her. After all, I was the one who was supposed to be doing that.

"That's okay, honey. I'll do it," she said, giving me a kiss on the forehead. "Why don't you go and relax a little bit. I know I've been keeping you pretty busy. You go enjoy yourself."

I ran back upstairs to the hall phone, but of course Emily was on it. Her bedroom door was shut, and the phone cord snaked out from under it. She was probably talking to Reed, which meant that she would be on forever. I knocked softly and called out, "Emily?" She opened the door, and I saw that she was still talking on the phone.

"Okay, Reed," she said into the receiver, holding up her finger to me. "So, I'll see you tomorrow, then. Bye."

Hanging up, Emily looked at me. "Hi, Katie," she said. "I'm glad you're here."

"You are?" I asked. I mean, she had been ignoring me and Mom, too, for that matter, for practically a whole month. What had happened?

"Yes, I wanted to talk to you about the wedding," Emily said, tossing her hair off one shoulder. She seemed like she was in a good mood for the first time since Mom and Jean-Paul had announced their engagement.

"Everything has to go very smoothly," Emily continued. "It's Mom's day, and it has to be perfect."

"But . . . but . . ." I began and then paused. I didn't even know how to ask her why she wasn't upset anymore, since we had never talked about how she felt in the first place. Emily put the phone down on her desk and turned around to look at me.

"But what?" she wanted to know.

"I thought you weren't happy about the wedding," I blurted out, feeling very confused.

Taking a deep breath, Emily said, "I guess I wasn't. But now I realize it's for the best, Katie. I know it is. Mom is so happy. We only want what's best for her, don't we?"

I nodded, sitting down on Emily's bed. I did want Mom to be happy. But then why did I still feel so unsure about the whole thing?

"I'm sorry if I haven't been around these past few weeks," Emily added. "I know you've had to do a lot of the work."

All the work didn't even matter to me anymore. I was just relieved that finally Emily wanted to talk about all this stuff.

"That's okay," I told her.

"You know," Emily said, sitting down next to me, and putting her arm around my shoulders, "I really miss Dad.

"I twisted around to look at her, totally surprised. "You, too?"

She nodded. "I keep thinking of all the stuff he used to do with us. Remember the time —"

Emily broke off as Mom walked into the room, holding up two dresses.

"What do you girls think?" she asked distractedly. "Would Jean-Paul like this aqua dress better, or the pale blue?"

Emily and I looked at each other, and we both started cracking up. I knew she was thinking exactly the same thing I was: *How* were we supposed to know *what* Jean-Paul liked? But my mom's question didn't bother me a bit. It was good to know that Emily and I could still share a lot of good memories about Dad, no matter what Jean-Paul liked or didn't like!

The final week before the wedding flew by in a blur. The next thing I knew, it was Friday. The rehearsal and rehearsal dinner were that night, and the wedding was the next afternoon. My mom had kept Emily and me out of school so that we could be there to help when all our guests arrived.

"Dad! Mom!" my mother exclaimed as Grandma and Grandpa Ryan walked in the door late Friday morning. "It's great to see you!"

"Eileen!" my grandparents said at the same time. My grandfather kissed my mom on the cheek, and Grandma Ryan gave her a hug.

"This is so exciting," Grandma Ryan said. "When do we get to meet this mysterious Frenchman?"

"Tonight," my mother replied, smiling. "At the rehearsal dinner."

"I can't wait," Grandpa Ryan said. When he caught sight of Emily and me standing at the bottom of the stairs, he walked over and gave Emily a kiss, and put his hand behind my ear. Then he pulled it out and handed me a quarter.

"You've still got rich ears, Katie," he said with a laugh. Grandpa Ryan had been pulling quarters out of my ears for as long as I could remember. I used to think it was a pretty neat trick when I was seven or eight, but it just wasn't the same anymore. I didn't want to tell him that, though. It might hurt his feelings.

"Hi, Grandpa," I said, giving him a hug. Mom linked arms with Grandma Ryan and led her and Grandpa into the living room. Turning to glance at me over her shoulder, she suggested, "Girls, why don't you take your grandparents' bags up to Emily's room?"

After we had moved the suitcases, I went into my room. I had to get my stuff together quickly, because Grandpa's brother, Great-uncle Max, would be at our house soon, and he was staying in my room.

My mother's sister, Aunt Elizabeth, and her husband, Ted, were going to stay in the guest room, and our cousins Jessie and Mike were sleeping on the fold-out sofa in the family room. The couch in the living room would be my bed, and Emily had made plans to stay at her friend Sarah's house. I didn't want to think about what a horror show the house would be the following morning, before the wedding — we only have one bathroom.

Suddenly I heard my mother calling frantically for me. I rushed down the stairs with my nightgown and some clothes in my hands. Mom was standing right outside the living room at the foot of the stairs.

"I need you to run to the grocery store, Katie," she said, brushing my hair off my forehead distractedly. "I forgot to get rolls for lunch. Uncle Max is going to be here soon, and he's sure to be hungry."

"Okay, Mom," I said, taking the money she handed me. I ran back upstairs and threw my clothes in a little bag. I ran back downstairs and put the bag in the closet for later.

Actually, I was thankful to get out of the house for a while. It was about to become a total madhouse.

All the way to the store and back, I thought about the wedding. It was strange to admit that I was getting a little excited. How could I help it? It was the next day. I also had to admit that Emily's and my bridesmaid dresses were nice. They were ice-blue, with a sweetheart neckline, fitted bodice, and pouffy sleeves.

The skirts were pouffy, too, and they were tea-length, which meant they came midway down our calves. I had never worn a dress like this before.

By the time I got back to the house, everyone was there. Our house is always so ordered and everything, it was really a surprise to see all the bags and coats and things piled all over the front hall. When I brought the rolls into the kitchen, I saw that everyone was in there making lunch.

"Great, here's Katie!" Aunt Elizabeth exclaimed as I pushed open the kitchen door. Aunt Elizabeth is my favorite aunt. She looks a lot like my mom, except she's a little taller and heavier. Taking the bag of rolls from my hand, my aunt turned back to my mother and said, "Eileen, I'm so incredibly happy for you. I can't wait to meet Jean-Paul and Michel. They both sound wonderful."

"Oh, they are," Mom replied with a smile.

"And how are you doing, Katie?" Uncle Ted asked, giving me a kiss on the cheek.

"Fine, Uncle Ted," I told him. My mom smiled at me, saying, "I'd say she's better than fine. Did you know Katie was chosen to be captain of the hockey team next year?"

Everybody congratulated me. Uncle Ted seemed especially happy for me — he had played hockey with my dad in college. I was about to tell him all about the team, but then I realized that my uncle was busy looking at my mom's engagement ring.

"Jean-Paul must not be doing too bad," he commented. "That's a pretty big diamond."

"Ted!" Aunt Elizabeth exclaimed with a laugh. I couldn't help laughing, too. Even though this wedding was kind of a pain, it was really nice to have the whole family around.

Chapter Seven

"Girls, would you like tea or milk?" Mom asked, as Emily and I walked into the kitchen late Friday afternoon.

"Tea, please," Emily replied, sitting down at the kitchen table. It was pretty crowded around the table, with Mom, Grandma Ryan, and Aunt Elizabeth, plus Emily and me. Mom had collected us all so we could review the schedule for tomorrow.

"I'll have milk," I said, going to the refrigerator and getting it myself. Actually, going over the schedule wasn't as complicated as I had thought it would be. I like things to be organized, and it was kind of nice figuring out who was doing what and where.

All the ladies, as my mom said, had to get their hair done at the beauty parlor the next morning, and then the photographer was coming to the house to take some pictures before the ceremony. The limos would arrive at our house by eleven-thirty to pick us up, and we had to be prompt.

After we went over some other small details I asked, "Mom, do you mind if I check things out in the attic now?" I had been meaning to go up there all week but hadn't gotten around to it. I had to do something about that dance now, or I never would.

"What things?" my mother asked. "Katie, the rehearsal's less than two hours away."

"The sixties dance," I replied. I guess I shouldn't have been surprised that she had forgotten about it. I hadn't mentioned the dance since the night she and Jean-Paul had announced their engagement. And she'd had a lot of other things on her mind since then.

"Oh, right," Mom said. "I packed most of that stuff in those boxes marked 'clothes.' They should be right near the top of the stairs. Just be careful up there. And don't get too dusty."

I nodded and headed up the stairs. I doubted that I was going find any clothes even half as wild as Mrs. Wells's. I couldn't picture my mother in anything like those bell-bottoms or velvet dress, and especially not in go-go boots.

The boxes were right where my mom had said they were, of course. I sat down and opened the first one. "Wow!" I exclaimed, looking down at the tie-dyed T-shirt on top.

Whatever I had expected to find in these boxes, this was not it.

Had Mom been a flower child? No way! I could not imagine that. But as I dug deeper, I found beaded headbands, fringed boots and ponchos, round wire-rimmed sunglasses, peace-sign earrings, and ripped, faded jeans. This box had to be in the wrong house.

I was giggling to myself by the time I opened the second box. It was more of the same. At the bottom I found a shoe box, which I dug out and set in my lap, popping the top off. It was full of snapshots, ticket stubs, and other mementos. Flipping through the photos, I couldn't believe it! There was my dad with long hair and a beard, standing in front of a VW van, with his arm around a young woman who was holding up two fingers in a peace sign. I looked closely. The woman was my mother! She was wearing a long, long skirt and an old work shirt with embroidery all over it. Her hair was really long, parted in the middle, and she had a beaded headband around her head. She wasn't wearing any shoes. My dad had on a tie-dyed shirt over patched jeans and wore rope sandals on his feet.

This was so cool! My parents had actually been hippies. I looked at the pictures for a long time before turning to the last of the three boxes. It was full of old albums — the Doors, Janis Joplin, Jimi Hendrix, Jefferson Airplane.

This was another total shock. I had always thought my mother was born listening to Glen Campbell. Grabbing the shoe box, I headed downstairs. I had to ask my mom about this. I was really surprised to find her alone. She was in her bedroom, with a mostly filled suitcase on her bed. I forgot that she had to pack for her honeymoon on top of everything else. I really don't know how she managed to keep everything straight.

"Did you find anything you could use, Katie?" she asked. Then she caught sight of the shoe box, and her hand flew to her mouth. "Oh, my goodness! I forgot those pictures were up there."

I put the box down on her bed and sat down next to it. "Was this really you?" I asked, pulling out the photo of her and my dad next to the VW van. Mom came over and sat next to me.

"I'm afraid so," she said with a little laugh. "It seems so long ago."

She began sifting through the other pictures. "I remember our first date. Your father took me to a peace rally," she said, looking at a snapshot of my dad with sideburns, long hair, and a paisley shirt. "He was something else. Everyone on campus knew who he was. He was always organizing a protest over something. All the girls were crazy about him."

"I didn't know you were involved with those protests," I said. It was wild to be discovering this whole different side to my mother.

"Oh, I wasn't," my mom said with a smile. "At least, not until I met your father. He had a way of being able to talk anybody into anything. He was so passionate about things, especially causes he thought were important."

I knew that was true. I could still remember how my dad had gotten really upset when there was talk about tearing down one of Acorn Falls' parks to put in a supermarket. He organized a protest outside of City Hall and wrote a bunch of letters to the local paper and everything.

They never did build that supermarket.

"We were so young then," my mom continued, flipping through the photos. "My goodness. Your father had so much energy. I remember, he didn't sleep the entire time we were at Woodstock."

I almost fell off the bed! "*You* went to Woodstock?"

My mom laughed. "Can you believe it?" she asked with a wry grin. "And now I'm working in a bank. Your father used to think it was really funny that we ended up in Acorn Falls in this house."

"Why?" I asked, looking around my mom's bedroom. I happen to think our house is really nice. My mom didn't answer right away. She finished sifting through the photos, then put them back in the box.

"Well," she said at last, "we had always talked about joining the Peace Corps after graduating from college."

"The Peace Corps?" I asked in astonishment. I couldn't see my mom doing that.

"That's right," she replied, nodding. "But then we decided to get married first. And right before we graduated, we found out we were going to have a baby."

"Emily," I said. I wondered if my sister knew about any of this. She was going to die when she found out. Mom nodded again.

"Right. And so we decided to stay. We moved back here, where your father had grown up, and bought this house. And we've been here ever since."

"Did you ever wish you'd joined the Peace Corps?" I asked. I couldn't help wondering if Emily and I had interrupted these big plans.

"Oh, no!" Mom exclaimed, putting her arm around me. "We never regretted our decision. Your father and I were so proud of you and Emily. We knew we had done the right thing by staying here. You girls made him so happy."

We sat there for a moment in silence. I thought about my dad. Sometimes I still couldn't believe he was gone. I expected him to come barging through the door and boom out that he was home. Then he'd go pick my mom up and swing her around.

"I miss Dad," I said softly. Mom stroked my hair.

"I know, honey," she replied. "I do, too. Every day."

"Then how can you marry Jean-Paul?" I asked before I could stop myself.

To my surprise, my mom didn't seem all that upset at my question.

"I love him," she replied calmly. "He's very different from your father, but I have a feeling that your father would have liked Jean-Paul."

I thought about that for a minute. "I think you're right, Mom," I finally said. "I think Dad would have liked him, too." Suddenly I just knew that everything was going to be okay. And I realized how important it was to me that Mom be happy.

Chapter Eight

On the day of the wedding, I woke up to silence. I couldn't believe it. It was quiet in my house for the first time since what felt like forever. I looked at my watch, which I had placed on the arm of the living room sofa after making up my bed the night before. It was just after six o'clock, so I crossed my arms behind my head and just lay there for a minute, enjoying the silence.

Thhia place had been a complete madhouse since all the relatives had shown up. Not that I wasn't happy to have them there — it was great to see everyone. It was just that things had gotten so disrupted over the last few weeks. I couldn't wait for this wedding to be over so that I could have my own room back and establish my routine again.

Then the thought of something else made me sit up in shock. There was no way I could go

74

back to the same routine! Jean-Paul and Michel were moving into our house when Mom and Jean-Paul came back from France.

Nothing would ever be the same again. I couldn't even be sure I would have the same room, since we had never talked about which room would be whose. I had just assumed I'd keep mine, and Michel would get the guest room. I certainly hoped so. I had had my room for as long as I could remember.

I swung my feet over the edge of the couch and stretched. I looked over the back of the sofa and out the window. The sun was shining in a clear, blue sky. It was definitely going to be a nice day. I knew that would make my mom really happy. She had been up listening to weather reports until past midnight last night.

Before anyone else got the same idea, I decided to hit the shower. Standing up, I folded all of my blankets and put them in the hall closet. Then I grabbed my bathrobe and headed for the bathroom upstairs. It would be great not to wait in line. Last night, trying to get into the bathroom before the rehearsal dinner had been impossible. I felt as if we should have gotten one of those things like they have in bakeries that gives out numbers. I didn't have to wash my hair, since we were all getting our hair done after breakfast, so I was in and out of the shower in a few minutes. I decided to dress in the bathroom. I put on comfortable jeans and a cotton sweater.

I thought about the rehearsal dinner the night before. It had actually gone very well. My mom had had us run through the whole ceremony in the church before we went over to Chez Pierre to eat.

Seeing what was going to happen made the wedding much more real to me. I had even gotten kind of excited about the whole thing. And meeting the whole Beauvais family was really intense. They had all come down from Canada for the wedding. I couldn't believe how many cousins Michel had. It seemed like there were dozens of them! I had totally lost track of who was who, so I hoped they wouldn't expect me to remember everyone's names today. I would have to ask Michel to tell me again, if we had time before the wedding.

I still couldn't get used to the fact that Michel and I were going to be part of the same family soon — in a matter of hours actually. I mean, it was weird enough to think of Jean-Paul and my mom getting married. But Michel as my brother? I could not imagine that at all. Shaking my head at my reflection in the medicine cabinet mirror, I gathered up my stuff and went out into the hall.

"My, you're up early," Grandma Ryan said, coming out of Emily's room and shutting the door behind her. "Couldn't sleep, Katie?"

"Morning, Grandma," I told her. "It's too nice a day to spend sleeping."

"I'm so glad the weather's good," Grandma said, smiling. "Your mother's going to be relieved. She was worried. Of course, in my day it was considered good luck for the bride if it rained on her wedding day. Nowadays brides just want sun."

I couldn't imagine what would be lucky about getting all soaked on your wedding day.

"What time is our hair appointment?" Grandma asked, changing the subject.

"Ten o'clock," I replied, smiling. That was another thing I was getting kind of excited about. I'd never had my hair done before. As Grandma disappeared into the bathroom, I went downstairs and poured myself a bowl of cereal.

I had just finished my cereal when the rush really began. It was hectic, what with everyone waiting for the bathroom and making coffee and eating breakfast. It seemed like there were people everywhere.

I wasn't sure when Emily arrived. Suddenly she was just there. Before I knew it, my mom was telling me it was time to go to the beauty parlor.

"Grandma, Aunt Elizabeth, Cousin Jessie, and Emily are already in the car," she said. "We'll drop off your things at Sabrina's on the way. Are you all packed?" I nodded, pointing to the duffel by the front door. I'd packed it the day before. Twenty minutes later, my bag was safely at Sabs's and we'd arrived at Betty Jean's Cut and Curl Beauty Parlor.

"Eileen!" Betty Jean called out as we walked in. "Today's the day! Sit right down, ladies. We're here to make you beautiful. You are getting the full treatment, right?" Mom nodded, and all of the sudden I began to wonder what I was in for. *The full treatment?* What was that? I thought we were just getting our hair done.

"Well, let's get started," Mom said, smiling at all of us. She, Emily, Aunt Elizabeth, Cousin

Jessie, and Grandma calmly walked to chairs and sat down. They actually looked happy at the thought of getting a "full treatment." Nervously I went over and sat down in a chair next to my mom. I wondered what they were going to do to me.

There were bottles of makeup and brightly colored jars all over every countertop. Not too many of them had labels. I wondered how Betty Jean and the other beauticians knew what was in them. What if they made a mistake and put something on me that they didn't mean to?

"My name's Donna," a big-haired woman with high heels said as she spun my chair around. "Let's get to work, dear."

"Work?" I echoed hesitantly as Donna fastened a cloth around my neck that fell over my clothes to protect them.

"Let's start with your hair," Donna said. "Come on over to the sink." I stood up and followed Donna to the sinks in the back. This is always my favorite part of getting my hair cut. I love sitting in those chairs that tilt back and having someone else wash my hair. It's really relaxing. The next thing I knew, she was tapping my shoulder.

"Okay, dear," she said, wrapping a towel around my dripping-wet hair. "You're all set."

Walking back to my chair, I watched Betty Jean putting curlers in my mom's hair. My mother looked really calm as she chatted with Betty Jean, watching her reflection in the mirror. One thing about beauty parlors that I don't like is all the mirrors. I mean, I know you need them to see what's being done to you, but I always feel really self-conscious. Once I was sitting down, there was nowhere else to look, though, so I stared straight ahead at my reflection.

"You've got really great hair," Donna said as she combed my wet hair out. "And great bone structure." She must say that to everyone who comes in, I figured. I mean, I know I'm not bad-looking, but I'm not model material or anything. Emily's the one with the great bone structure and perfect hair. I'm just . . . Katie.

"Ouch!" I yelped, before I could stop myself. Donna had taken out these pink rubber tube things and was curling the ends of my hair around them. I guess she had caught one of those little hairs near my scalp. It hurt.

"Sorry, dear," Donna apologized, without pausing. After my hair was all rolled up in those pink rubber tubes, or twisties, as Donna called them, she led me over to the row of hair dryer helmets against the opposite wall. I couldn't hear anything with that thing over my head, but it was kind of relaxing that way.

I kind of tensed when I saw Donna wheel a white cart and stool over in front of me. What was she going to do now? I must have looked a little nervous, because Donna smiled and held up a bottle of nail polish. I figured that Mom had probably come over here earlier to pick out the color — it looked like it was going to complement my dress perfectly. There really are a lot of details to be worked out in a wedding.

The next thing I knew, my hands were soaking in this little bowl on top of the cart. I wondered what for and looked over at Emily, who was sitting under the dryer helmet next to mine.

"To soften your cuticles," Emily said. She looked as if she were talking really loudly, but with the sound of the dryers I barely heard her. I nodded, even though I wasn't sure why my cuticles had to be softened in order for my nails to be painted. But it didn't matter. It actually felt kind of good. Soon my hair was dry and my nails had been cut, filed, and polished.

Donna told me not to move my hands for the next fifteen minutes or I might smudge a nail, so I sat as motionless as possible for the next fifteen minutes.

Emily walked around the room, waving her hands around while her nails dried, too.

"Mother, your hair looks great!" Emily exclaimed, going to stand behind Mom. "You look so young!"

"Weddings suit you," Aunt Elizabeth added. "Eileen, you look terrific." Mom blushed a little.

"Thank you," she replied. "Betty Jean did a wonderful job."

"Well, I had great material to work with," Betty Jean said.

Mom did look fantastic. I couldn't wait to see her all finished, in her pale pink dress. Blush-colored, Emily called it. But it looked like plain old pale pink to me.

"Okay, dear," Donna suddenly said to me. "Let's get going. We've still got a lot of work ahead of us."

I didn't like all this talk about work, but I dutifully sat down in my chair in front of the mirror again. Donna began pulling the twisties out of my hair. When she was finished, my hair fell in soft, blond waves around my face. It looked so nice I almost couldn't believe it was really my hair.

"Looks perfect, dear," Donna said, grinning. "I told you you had great hair. Now sit back and let me get to work on your face."

She pulled out a jar and a big brush. I watched everything warily. I mean, she *had* done a great job on my hair, but who knew what else the "full treatment" meant. It was kind of hard to make sense of what she was doing, though, since I never wear makeup.

When she was finished, I gasped, staring at my reflection. My eyes looked incredibly big and blue, with a touch of pale blue eye shadow on the lids and some bluish-gray color lining them. She'd dusted my cheeks with blush and then applied some sort of pink, shimmery gloss to my lips. I looked so different and glamorous with all those blond waves falling around my face.

"Katie, you look beautiful," Mom said, coming up behind my chair and putting her hands on my shoulders.

"Thanks, Mom," I said softly. I didn't want to disturb my hair or anything. It looked too perfect. My friends were going to die when they saw me. Suddenly I started getting really excited about the wedding. I just couldn't wait to see how I looked in my dress!

Chapter Nine

My friends were already there when we got back to my house. They were in the living room talking to Uncle Ted and Grandpa Ryan. I hoped Grandpa hadn't been pulling quarters out of their ears.

"Katie, I'm so excited," Sabs said, jumping up as soon as she saw me. "Let's go put your dress right on —" She stopped in the middle of her sentence, then exclaimed, "Wow! You look just like the model on the cover of this month's *Young Chic.*"

"I really like your hair," said Al as she and Randy got up from the couch.

"Awesome makeup job," Randy added. "You should wear that stuff all the time."

I grinned at my friends. "Thanks, you guys. And thanks for coming over to help me."

Just then my mom came in. After my friends had said hello and met all my relatives, we headed up to my room.

"You guys look really nice, too," I told them as I opened the door to my room and we went inside. Sabs looked down at her shimmery blue-green drop-waisted dress with spaghetti straps, which she was wearing with elbow-length lace gloves that were cut off at the fingers.

"Really? Do you think this is dressy enough for a wedding?" she asked.

"Definitely," Randy told her. Randy had on a black-and-white top that had a sailor collar and was nipped in at the waist. Then it flared out over a matching black miniskirt. It was kind of like a sailor suit, but really elegant.

Al's dress had a black velvet top and a puffy pink satin skirt with a wide band of velvet near the waist of the skirt and around the bottom. The middle section was pink satin. She wore a really wide black velvet headband with it. Looking around my room, Randy asked, "Where should we start, Katie?"

"Look at your bridesmaid dress!" Sabs cried. She rushed over to where it was hanging on the outside of my closet door.

"You have to put this on right away." Ten minutes later, I was in total shock as I stared at my reflection in the mirror. I could not believe the girl in that beautiful dress was really me.

"You look like something out of a fairy tale," Al said softly. She, Randy, and Sabs were clustered right behind me. Suddenly I started feeling nervous. I mean, in just an hour I was going to be in my mom's wedding! What if something went wrong?

"Are you all right, Katie?" Randy asked, putting her hand on my shoulder. "I mean, is the wedding still bothering you? You can tell us."

I smiled nervously at them. "No, I'm fine about my mom and Jean-Paul and everything. It's just that I want everything to be perfect. What if I trip on my way down the aisle? What if my hair gets mussed or —"

"There's no way that's going to happen," Sabs cut in firmly. "We're going to make sure of it." She grabbed my brush from the dresser, kicked off her shoes, and jumped up on my bed.

"Come over here so I can fix your hair," said Sabs. It had gotten a teeny little bit messed from putting on the dress.

"What about flowers?" Randy asked. "Aren't you going to be carrying any?" I was pretty sure my mom had all the flowers down-stairs, so Randy went to get mine.

Meanwhile, Allison pulled over this little stool I have and sat on it, smoothing my skirt. Since my bridesmaid dress had that pouffy skirt, it was really important that it fall correctly.

"Perfect!" Al, Sabs, and Randy all declared at once, a while later. By the time we all went downstairs I was feeling a lot better. I was really happy Mom let my friends stay and watch while the photographer took shots of all of us in the living room.

Soon it was time to leave for the church. It was just a few blocks from my house, so Sabs, Randy, and Al were going to walk there.

. When we got to the church, Sabs gave me a hug at the door, being careful not to mess any-thing up.

"Don't worry. Everything's going to go great," Sabs said.

"See you after the ceremony," Randy added with a wave. "If you get nervous, just look for us."

Then Al added, "It will help calm you down." I waved as they ran through the door, positive that I had the best friends in the world.

"Katie, you look *fantastique!*" Michel whispered to me as we walked into the vestibule of the church.

"Merci," I whispered back with a smile. I felt fantastic, too. It was nice that he thought I looked the way I felt, especially since it doesn't always work out that way.

"So do you!" I added. And he did. Sabs was going to die when she saw Michel. He looked awesome in his tuxedo. Michel was one of the ushers. He had to lead people into their seats in the church. The left side of the church was reserved for friends and family of the bride, he told me, while the right was for friends and family of the groom. I wondered where you were supposed to sit if you were friends with both.

Anyway, he had just led Grandma Ryan down the aisle to the front pew. She was the last person to be seated before we started the procession. The church was pretty full.

Seeing all those people who kept looking expectantly toward the vestibule, where we were waiting, I was starting to get a little nervous — especially since Michel and I were going to be the first two people to walk down the aisle. Just then I heard the first strains of music coming from the organ in the front of the church. I knew from last night's rehearsal that it was time to start.

Jean-Paul stepped out from a door at the front of the church, up near the organ. His friend Mark Mitterand was right behind him. Mr. Mitterand was the best man. They stood together at the end of the aisle. Jean-Paul looked great in his tuxedo. I had never realized before how much he and Michel look alike.

Michel turned and whispered to me, "It's time." He took my hand and gave it a quick squeeze. I think he knew I was a little nervous. Then he put my hand in the crook of his elbow, like my mom had shown us the night before.

"Don't rush," Emily whispered to me. She was standing right behind me. She and Jean-Paul's cousin Philippe would be walking down the aisle together next. "Just take your time, Katie," Emily whispered to me.

I nodded, and then Michel and I took our first step down the aisle.

Mom had shown us how to count so we walked really slowly. I could hear Michel counting in French under his breath, "*Un, deux, trois,*" before he took another step. Everyone in the church turned around and faced us. It was a little weird with everyone watching. But then I spotted Sabs, Randy, and Allison. They all smiled at me. Sabs started waving, and I saw her eyes get really big when she saw Michel.

We got to the end of the aisle without any major catastrophe or anything. Michel had to go stand on the right side, and I had to stand on the left, next to these special chairs that had been set up for the wedding party in front of all the pews. Michel winked at me and squeezed my hand again just before we split up. Then I was standing in front of my seat, watching Emily and Philippe walk the rest of the way down the aisle.

Aunt Elizabeth was next. She walked slowly and held herself very straight. I think she was probably afraid of messing up her hair or something. It's really long, and Betty Jean had piled it all up on top of her head. It looked great, but I just hoped a strong wind wouldn't hit it when we walked outside after the ceremony. Aunt Elizabeth might topple right over!

Everyone in the church stood up, and then all these cameras started flashing. I knew my mom must have started walking down the aisle, but I couldn't see her over the heads of all the people standing. The next thing I knew, my mom was going right past me, walking with Grandpa Ryan. She looked incredible. Her blush-colored dress was similar in style to Emily's and mine, but it had an overlay of chiffon, so it swirled around her as she walked. Mom looked so happy.

I knew in that one instant that this wedding really was the right thing for her.

When Mom reached the end of the aisle, Grandpa gave her a kiss on the cheek and then gave her hand over to Jean-Paul. I could hear Jean-Paul say, "Thank you," to Grandpa, and then he and Mom faced forward while Grandpa went over to sit with Grandma in the first pew.

The ceremony was really nice. There were a lot of readings and music. Before I knew it, my mom and Jean-Paul exchanged rings and the minister was saying something about "man and wife." And then Jean-Paul was kissing Mom and everyone was taking pictures again.

A few seconds later, the rest of us were following them back down the aisle toward the rear of the church. When Michel and I got back out to the vestibule, Jean-Paul and Mom were already lined up with Aunt Elizabeth, Mr. Mitterand, Philippe, and Emily. I walked over and gave Mom and Jean-Paul a quick hug and then got in line between Philippe and Michel.

We all had to stand there while everyone poured out of the church so they could congratulate us. It took a long time for the church to empty out. Actually, it felt as if it took even longer than the ceremony itself!

"Katie!" Sabs exclaimed, coming over to give me a hug. "The wedding was awesome. Your mom looks incredible, and Jean-Paul is so handsome. Everything was so beautiful. I almost cried."

"You did cry," Randy said with a laugh, as she and Allison walked up behind Sabs. Then Al and Randy both hugged me.

"Well, maybe I cried a little," Sabs admitted. "But not a lot. Anyway, it was so beautiful, I don't know how you didn't cry, Randy."

Randy laughed again. "I guess I'm just not the crying type," she said. "But it was really nice. How are you doing, Katie?" I just grinned at her. I was doing great. Everything had gone so well. My mom was smiling and laughing on my other side, and Jean-Paul had his arm around her. I didn't know how to explain how fantastic all of those things made me feel, so I didn't say anything. Anyway, I think my friends understood, because they all grinned back at me.

"You did great going down the aisle," Al told me. "You didn't look a bit nervous."

"Michel, I love your tuxedo," Sabs gushed, turning to him.

"*Merci*," he said, and then he leaned over and gave her a peck on the cheek. Of course Sabs turned bright red.

"So, I guess we'll see you over at the reception," Randy said, looking at her watch. "You have to get photos taken or something, right?"

I nodded. "It shouldn't take too long, though," I said. "At least, I hope not. I'm starving!"

Sabs grabbed Randy and Al by the arm. "Come on, you guys, let's get going. My dad is probably waiting for us outside to drive us over. I can't wait to see the country club!"

I waved happily to my friends as they bounced down the steps of the church. It was strange, but I felt as sunny as the weather.

Chapter Ten

When we got to the Acorn Falls Country Club, the photographer and his assistant led everyone in the wedding party into a back banquet room that was filled with flowers. It felt like they took tons and tons of pictures, but I think it was only about six rolls.

Then we had to line up again the way we had walked down the aisle, to walk into the reception room. I could hear a band playing — another thing Mom had had to organize! The drummer did a little drum roll, and then the manager from the country club picked up a microphone.

"Ladies and gentlemen," he said, "I'd like to introduce the wedding party to you." Everyone quieted down, and Michel took my hand and put it in the crook of his arm again.

"Ready, K.C.?" he asked.

"*Oui*," I told him, nodding.

"Bridesmaid Katherine Campbell and usher Michel Beauvais!" the manager announced. Michel and I walked into the room toward to the head table.

Everyone clapped and whistled. We walked faster than we had at the church, so we were there in a flash. While the others were being introduced, I looked around the reception hall. It was huge, with a big crystal chandelier, a dance floor, and windows all along one wall looking out over the golf course. All the tables looked really nice, with white tablecloths, candles, flowers, and several different glasses on them.

After Aunt Elizabeth and Mr. Mitterand had been introduced, everyone stopped clapping and was quiet. In a hushed tone, the manager said, "And, introducing for the first time, Mr. and Mrs. Jean-Paul Beauvais!" Mom and Jean-Paul walked in, and everyone went crazy, clapping and cheering. Mom looked so happy that she seemed as if she was about to cry. Once we were all standing at the end table, everyone sat down, except Mr. Mitterand. As best man, he had to make the first toast to the new couple.

I was really glad that Mom had gone over

everything the night before, or I wouldn't have had a clue about what was going on. After all, this was the first wedding I had ever been to. Mark gave the toast in French and in English. Then everyone clapped again and started tapping their champagne glasses with their forks. I leaned over and asked Emily, "Why are they doing that? What if someone breaks a glass?"

Emily laughed. "It's to make Mother and Jean-Paul kiss," she explained.

"Why?" I asked.

"I don't know," Emily admitted. "But it's a tradition." Talk about weird. But then again, I wasn't an expert on weddings or anything, so I just picked up my fork and tapped it against my glass like everyone else. All through dinner, people kept on tapping their glasses, and Mom and Jean-Paul had to keep kissing. I thought it was kind of embarrassing, but they didn't seem to mind at all.

After a while dinner was over, and the waiters cleared away our dinner plates. Jean-Paul stood up and led Mom to the dance floor.

"What's going on now?" I asked Emily.

"The bride and groom are supposed to dance the first dance together, by themselves,"

Aunt Elizabeth told me. "Then the rest of us in the wedding party dance the second dance with them.

I started to feel nervous all over again. "I have to dance?" I asked. No one had mentioned that to me. I mean, I know how to dance — but not this waltzing stuff Mom and Jean-Paul were doing.

"Don't worry, K.C.," said Michel. "My father made me take ballroom dance lessons when I was in fourth form. I will lead, so we will be fine. Just follow what I do."

I nodded, but kept my eyes glued to Mom and Jean-Paul. It looked a little more complicated than that. I tried to follow them and see what they were doing, but it didn't make much sense to me. Then the song ended, and the band leader walked over to the microphone and said into it, "Will the wedding party join our happy couple on the floor, please?"

I took a deep breath as Michel took my hand and led me down to the dance floor. At first I just stood there facing him, not sure what to do. Then Michel grabbed my hands and arranged things so that I was holding his shoulder with my left hand, and he was holding my waist.

Then he clasped my right hand in his left, holding it up a little.

"*Ça va?*" he asked. I nodded, even though I definitely did not feel okay. I didn't feel as if I had a handle on what was going on.

"Now we will count to four," he instructed. "We are going to move in a box shape. And you will follow my lead."

I could tell Michel was taking it all very seriously, but I couldn't help myself. Suddenly I started giggling.

"What is so funny?" he asked.

"This is the only time you could say, 'Follow my lead,' and I would," I said, with another giggle.

"That is true," Michel replied, grinning. "I hope it is a long song."

When the music started, Michel started moving in his box shape, and I tried to follow him without stepping on his feet. I have to admit, I had to keep looking down to make sure I was going the right way. And it took a lot to concentrate on the four-count. It was really hard work.

After the song ended, everyone wanted to dance. I danced with my grandfather, Jean-Paul,

Mr. Mitterand, Philippe, Michel again, and a bunch of Canadian relatives I couldn't name.

My mom danced with practically every man in the room. I never thought I would get the hang of waltzing, but after a while I actually started enjoying it.

Finally the band took a rest, and I was able to get over to my friends' table.

"Hi, guys," I said, slipping into the empty chair next to Allison. "My feet are killing me."

"You've been dancing a lot," Sabs said. "I didn't even know you knew how to waltz."

"I don't," I admitted with a giggle. "You're just supposed to follow the guy's lead. I really wish they'd play something we could dance to, though."

Randy nodded. "Me, too. But I'm sure we'll get enough dancing in tonight."

"I forgot all about the sixties dance!" I exclaimed."

"It's no wonder with all of this going on," Allison said, taking a sip of her ice water.

"Well, it's no problem if you need to borrow some of my mom's clothes," Sabs reassured me.

I shook my head. "Mom had a bunch of stuff," I told Sabs. "She was actually really into all that sixties stuff."

Sabs's hazel eyes went wide, and she exclaimed, "You're kidding!" Then she giggled and said, "Though I guess if my mom used to wear red, white, and blue bell-bottoms, anything is possible!"

"So what are you going to wear?" Randy asked me.

I had picked out a great outfit, but I thought it would make abigger impact if I didn't describe it first. "It's a surprise," I replied. "You guys are going to die!"

Sabs looked as if she was going to object, but then she froze, staring at something over my shoulder.

"Ohmygosh! I think your mom's going to cut the cake now!" We stood up and moved to the edge of the dance floor as they wheeled out a huge white cake with a miniature bride and groom on top. Mom and Jean-Paul walked over with a big knife. Randy started giggling, and I didn't even have to ask to know that she was thinking about horror movie scenes. Then Mom and Jean-Paul cut the cake together. Mom had to feed a piece to Jean-Paul and then he had to feed Mom.

"At my cousin Simon's wedding, he smushed the cake all over Angie's face," Sabs whispered. "It was really funny." Luckily for my mom, Jean-Paul didn't smush her piece. After they cut the cake, the waiters started carrying it around to all the tables.

"I'm just going to grab my cake," I said to my friends. "Then I'll meet you back at your table."

Michel was sitting in his chair when I took my piece of cake and started back toward my friends.

"K.C., where are you going?" he asked.

"To sit with Sabs, Al, and Randy," I told him.

Michel pressed his lips together, and this really serious look came into his dark eyes. "Do you think I should ask Sabrina to dance when the music starts again?" he asked.

I had forgotten that he kind of has a crush on Sabs, even though they've never been out on a date or anything. "Definitely," I replied.

Pretty soon the band started up again, and this time they were playing faster music. It wasn't rock and roll or anything, but at least we could fast-dance to it.

Sabs was totally excited when Michel asked

her to dance. And then all his Canadian relatives started coming over to me and my friends and asking us to dance. I still had no idea who was who, but at least they were starting to look familiar. We hardly sat down for the rest of the afternoon.

The reception lasted four hours, but it felt like four minutes, it flew by so fast. Before I knew it, everyone was getting ready to go. Mom and Jean-Paul came over to me and gave me hugs and kisses. They were heading right for the plane from there.

"Now, you're going to be all right at the Wellses', Katie?" my mom asked. She actually had tears in her eyes, and I had to blink to keep from getting a little teary myself.

"Don't worry about a thing, Mom," I told her. "I'll be fine. You just concentrate on relaxing. You really need a vacation."

Mom smiled at me and then at Jean-Paul. "I sure do, honey," she said. "But I'll miss you."

"*Moi aussi*," Jean-Paul agreed. "I will miss you, too, Katie."

"I'll call you tomorrow to let you know we got to France safe and sound," Mom said, giving me another hug.

"Okay, Mom," I said. "See you when you get back!"

"Love you, honey," she said. And then she and Jean-Paul were gone. I watched them walk out of the reception hall, and I knew that things would never be the same again. But somehow it didn't matter. Glancing at Michel and Emily joking around with Reed, I knew things would be okay, maybe even better than ever. We were going to be a family! It was a weird thought, but a good one.

I was smiling as I turned around to find my friends. We had to get a move on. We had a dance to get ready for, and we were running out of time!

Chapter Eleven

"Randy, you look great!" I said, looking up from the latest issue of Sabs's favorite magazine, *Young Chic*, which I had been flipping through on her bed. Randy had just appeared in Sabs's room, wearing a black, long-sleeved cat suit with the silver belt she had borrowed from Sabs slung around her hips. Her hair was held back with a thick black headband, and she was wearing rhinestone cat-eye glasses.

"You're not ready yet?" Randy asked, looking down at my bathrobe.

"Sabs is still in the bathroom," I said, with a grin. Sabs and Emily are a lot alike that way. I don't really understand what they do in there. I just go in, shower, and get out. No big deal.

"Oh, and Al just called. She's on her way over." Randy flopped down next to me on Sabs's bed. "So, your mom's gone?" Randy asked. "I can't believe they're going to the

French Riviera."

"Me, neither," I agreed. "You know, this is the first time I've ever been away from my mom for so long." I felt embarrassed as soon as the words were out of my mouth. I mean, Randy is always so totally independent.

"You probably think that's really babyish or something," I mumbled, looking down at my bare feet.

"I don't think it's babyish," Randy said right away. "It's a good thing you're staying with Sabs, then."

"Why?" I asked. I was glad I was staying with Sabs, too, but I didn't see what that had to do with missing my mom.

"Because she'll keep you so busy you probably won't even realize your mom's gone until she's back," Randy said, laughing. "That girl never sits still for a second."

"That's the truth!" I agreed.

Someone knocked lightly on the door to Sabs's room, and Randy yelled out, "Come on in!" Al poked her head in, hesitating for a moment before she pushed open the door.

"Al, you're perfect!" Randy exclaimed. The golden-yellow dress looked fantastic on her. In the short dress and go-go boots, her legs looked longer than ever, and her straight black hair was hanging loose down her back, swirling with her movements. She looked very sixties.

"Thanks," Al replied. "You look really good, too, Randy." Randy stood up and twirled around quickly. "M had it lying around," she said. "Pretty cool, huh?"

We all turned as Sabs came back upstairs, already dressed for the dance. "Guys, these bell-bottoms still feel really weird," Sabs said, grimacing. "I don't know how they wore them every day."

"I know what you mean," Al agreed, looking at her vinyl go-go boots. "I can barely walk in these."

Sabs gasped when she realized that I was still in my bathrobe. "Oh, Katie! I forgot you were going to take a quick shower."

"Don't worry about it," I reassured her. "I'll be very fast." I leaned over and picked up my duffel bag with my costume in it. "Be right back."

Running down to the second floor, I hopped into the shower. All that dancing at the reception had made me a little sweaty, although I was kind of sad to wash off my makeup. It felt great to be under the refreshing water. I quickly washed, rinsed, and dried off. Then I got into my sixties stuff. I couldn't stop myself from grinning when I looked at my reflection in the mirror. My friends were going to flip when they saw these clothes.

"Ohmygosh, Katie!" Sabs exclaimed as soon as I walked back upstairs. "Where did you get all that?" I was wearing a fringed, woven poncho that had a beaded design on it, over a tie-dyed shirt with a big peace sign on the front. My jeans were really old and ripped, and I had fringed suede moccasin boots over them that came up to my knees. I was also wearing a beaded headband around my head, long, dang-ly earrings, and a lot of different-colored beaded necklaces.

"It was my mom's," I said, grinning.

"No way!" Randy said, jumping up from the bed. "I don't believe it. Your mom was a flower child?"

I nodded, cracking up at how shocked my friends were. "Believe me, I was really sur-prised, too. I mean, she and my dad actually went to a peace rally on their first date. They were at Woodstock, *and* they were going to join the Peace Corps when they first got married."

"Totally, no way!" Randy said again. "They went to Woodstock?" I nodded.

"I think I like what you're wearing more than my outfit," Allison commented, pointing especially at my boots. I completely understood what she was talking about. Her vinyl boots had thick, stiff heels on them, and they made this plastic squeaking noise whenever she walked. They looked like they would be torture to have on for longer than thirty seconds.

"You mean to say you don't wish all your clothes were made out of vinyl?" Randy joked.

Just then Sabs's older brother Luke called up to the attic that if we didn't leave right now, he wasn't going to drive us. He can be a real tyrant when it comes to driving Sabs places.

"Let's rock-and-roll, you guys," Sabs said, grabbing her jacket. "Sam and Michel already left."

The school was all lit up when Luke stopped the car in front of the gym ten minutes later.

"You kids have fun," he said, turning around in his seat. Luke's only sixteen, but he gets a real kick out of calling Sabs and all of us kids. We're only three years younger than he is, after all. Of course, he acted like it was a total pain when Sabs arranged for a pickup at ten, after the dance. After Luke drove away, we walked inside the gym. We could hear the band playing all the way in the outside hall.

"Great tune!" Randy exclaimed. "I love Creedence Clearwater Revival!"

"Me, too!" Sabs agreed. Al and I exchanged looks. We aren't as up on music as Randy and Sabs are — or in this case, into music history. Shrugging, we followed Sabs and Randy inside. The gym looked really cool. Winslow's decorating committee had set up these colored lights that flicked on and off in time to the music. Very psychedelic. And there were peace signs and flower-power decorations everywhere.

Looking around, I kind of wondered where Michel was. I hadn't seen him since the reception. It was funny, the way he just kind of popped into my head. I never used to think about where he was or what he was doing. I guessed that would change now that we were going to be living in the same house.

"K.C.!" I heard someone call out behind me. I turned around and saw Scottie walking toward me. He was wearing a tie-dyed T-shirt and ripped-up jeans. I thought he looked really cute.

"You guys match!" Sabs whispered. "That must mean something." I don't believe in cosmic connections or anything, but I was really happy Scottie was coming over to talk to me.

"Listen, we'll be over by the punch, Katie," Allison said to me. "You can meet us over there."

"Okay," I replied as they walked away. Scottie stopped next to me and shoved his hands in his pockets.

"How are you doing, K.C.?" he asked. "How was your mom's wedding?"

"Good," I answered. "I like your shirt, Scottie."

He grinned at me. "I like yours, too," he said.

The band started playing "Wild Horses" by the Rolling Stones, and most of the kids cleared off the floor. It's funny how a slow song can do that. We stood there not saying anything for a second.

"Do you want to dance?" Scottie asked suddenly.

"Sure." Scottie took my hand and led me out

to the middle of the gym. I could not believe I was going to slow-dance with Scottie Silver.

Sabs was going to die. She always says slow dancing is so romantic, but I had always avoided it before. I'm not sure why. I guess I just hadn't felt comfortable about it until now. I had to stifle a giggle, thinking about all the slow dancing I'd already done that day. I hoped that Scottie didn't expect me to waltz or anything. I had had enough of that for one day. He didn't. He just put his hands on my waist and I put mine around his neck, and we sort of moved back and forth to the music. I don't know if it was romantic exactly, but slow dancing with Scottie was definitely kind of nice.

Suddenly I saw Michel standing behind Scottie. He didn't look happy. In fact, he was glaring at Scottie.

"Do you mind if I cut in?" Michel asked in this stiff voice.

"Hey, Beauvais!" Scottie said, smiling at Michel over his shoulder. "How's it going? Listen, you probably danced with K.C. a lot at the wedding. It's my turn now, okay?"

"I would really like to dance with her again," Michel persisted, still glaring at Scottie.

I felt really uncomfortable, so I stepped a little away from Scottie. Talk about embarrassing! What was with Michel? Couldn't he see that I was perfectly happy dancing with Scottie? I really did not want to dance with Michel at that moment.

"I am going to cut in," Michel continued. Scottie stepped back and held up his hands. "Fine," he said, rolling his eyes at me. "No skin off my back, man." Michel watched him go and then turned to me and held up his hands. I could not believe Michel had been so rude to Scottie. And he didn't seem to care about what *I* wanted at all.

I was furious. Planting my hands on my hips, I glowered at Michel. "What are you doing?" I asked him. "I was dancing with Scottie."

"I know you were," Michel replied. "That is why I was worried. He dates many girls. I saw him last week with Jeanne Keller at Fitzie's."

"So what?" I asked, not really seeing what the point was. Scottie and I weren't married or anything. I liked Scottie, and he liked me. What was the big deal? I know Scottie has a lot of friends who are girls. "Besides, if it bugs you so much, how come you never said anything before?" I asked.

Being on the team and all, Michel had to have known that Scottie and I had gone to Fitzie's a couple of times. Those guys tell each other everything.

"You were not my sister before," Michel said in a very serious voice. "Now I have to look out for you." I was floored. He couldn't be serious.

"I can look after myself, thank you very much!" I said loudly. "I don't need you to do that for me!"

"But, K.C. — " Michel began.

"My mom and your dad have only been married for a few hours," I said, cutting him off. "And you're already acting like you have the right to tell me what I can do," I continued angrily. "Just leave me alone! I don't want to be your sister!"

Seeing my friends by the punch bowl, I stalked over to them. I couldn't believe Michel. The last thing I had expected when Mom had married Jean-Paul was a bodyguard for a brother.

"What's wrong, Katie?" Allison asked as I joined them at the punch bowl.

114

"Michel just cut in with me and Scottie because he said that he felt he had to look after me!" I fumed. "Who does he think he is? What gives him the right?"

Sabs laughed.

"What's so funny?" I demanded.

"Get used to it, Katie," she replied. "You've got a brother now."

"So?" I asked.

"Well, that's what brothers do," Sabs explained. "Believe me, I've got four. They think they have to look after you all the time and protect you and stuff."

I could not believe what she was telling me. "But he's no older than I am," I protested.

"It doesn't matter," Sabs replied. "Sam is the same way. I don't know why they act that way, but you're going to have to get used to it."

I took a couple of deep breaths, calming down a little. "But I don't know if I want to get used to it," I said.

"Brothers can be okay, too," Sabs said. "They have their good points."

"What?" I asked grudgingly. So far I had definitely not seen any.

"Well, sometimes it's nice to have someone

looking after you," Sabs explained. Randy nodded.

"Sabs has got a point," she agreed. "Sometimes I wish I had a brother."

"Really?" I asked, a little shocked.

"But the best thing about having brothers is . . ." Sabs began and then trailed off. She grinned at me.

"What?" I asked.

"Most of the time they have really cute friends!" Sabs finished. I cracked up at that. I mean, how could I not? That was definitely something to look forward to.

"What's Michel doing now?" Randy asked, pointing to the middle of the gym floor. Michel and Scottie were fooling around waltzing with each other. I couldn't believe it. Scottie had seemed pretty mad when he walked away before, but obviously neither of them was holding a grudge. "Let's go out there," Sabs said, pulling us onto the dance floor.

"Come on, guys, it'll be fun," Sabs added excitedly.

Stacy the Great Hansen and her friends were dancing right next to Scottie, Michel, and all the other guys from the hockey team.

Stacy is the principal's daughter, and she also happens to be one of the most stuck-up girls at Bradley. She and her friends were obviously trying very hard to get noticed by Scottie and Michel.

"Michel is so cute!" Stacy's friend Eva exclaimed, loud enough for us to hear.

"If you like babies," Stacy said with a toss of her long blond hair. "I prefer older men." Stacy had gone to the movies with a ninth grader the week before, and the whole school knew about it already. Stacy is really great at doing her own public relations. I saw Randy walk over to Stacy, and I knew she was going to say something. Randy can't help herself. She really likes to pick fights with Stacy, and she happens to be one of the few people who can really get Stacy's goat.

"Who are you calling a baby?" Randy asked.

Stacy gave Randy this haughty look, then replied, "It's none of your business. But boys who dance with each other are kind of juvenile. I mean, please."

"You're talking about my brother!" I jumped in angrily, before I could stop myself. It was the weirdest thing. Suddenly I got mad at Stacy for saying anything bad about Michel. I knew she didn't really mean it. She thinks Michel is really cute. I've heard her say his accent is awesome. But I still didn't want to hear her say anything bad about him.

"What are you talking about?" Stacy asked.

"What?" Michel asked at the same time.

"Don't say things like that about my brother!" I repeated firmly.

"Your brother?" Stacy retorted with a laugh. "Get real, Katie. Just because your mother married his father doesn't make you guys brother and sister."

The smug look on Stacy's face kind of fell as Michel went over to her, his dark eyes flashing angrily.

"There is one thing that I want you always to remember, Stacy Hansen," he said, pointing a finger at her. "K.C. *is* definitely my sister."

"That's right," I added, grinning up at Michel. "I'm his sister."

Sabs was right. I was going to have to get used to having Michel as my brother. I figured right now was as good a time as any to start.

Stacy didn't say anything. She just opened her mouth and shut it. Then she spun on her heel and stormed off. Her friends followed right behind.

I put my arm through Michel's, and we walked over to where Sabs, Al, and Randy were standing. Sabs gave us both a really big hug.

"You two really showed her!"

"I love it!" Randy agreed.

Allison smiled and said, "There's nothing like family. And yours is definitely a great one."

"Al, you're a mind reader," I said, beaming happily at Michel and my friends. I know it sounds corny, but I had to admit that this had been one of the coolest days of my whole life.

Look for these titles in the GIRL TALK series

1 WELCOME TO JUNIOR HIGH! Introducing the Girl Talk characters, Sabrina Wells, Katie Campbell, Randy Zak, and Allison Cloud. When our four heroines meet and have to plan the first junior high dance of the year, the results are hilarious.

2 FACE-OFF! Katie Campbell is just plain fed up with being "perfect." But when she decides to join the boys' ice hockey team, she gets more than she bargained for.

3 THE NEW YOU Allison Cloud's world turns upside down when she is chosen to model for *Belle* magazine with Stacy the Great!

4 REBEL, REBEL Randy Zak is acting even stranger than usual. Could a visit from her cute New York friend have something to do with it?

5 IT'S ALL IN THE STARS Sabrina gets even when she discovers that someone is playing a practical joke on her — and all her horoscopes are coming true.

6 THE GHOST OF EAGLE MOUNTAIN The girls go on a weekend ski trip, only to discover that they're sleeping on the very spot where the Ghost of Eagle Mountain wanders!

THE WINNING TEAM

☆13 It's a fight to the finish when Sabrina and Sam run against Stacy the great and Eva Malone for president and vice-president of the seventh grade!

EARTH ALERT!

☆14 Allison, Katie, Sabrina, and Randy try to convince Bradley junior high to turn the annual seventh grade fun fair into a fair to save the Earth!

ON THE AIR

☆15 Randy lands the after-school job of her dreams as the host of a one hour radio program. Trouble is, she becomes an overnight success and starts seeing Randy-clones where ever she goes!

HERE COMES THE BRIDE

☆16 There's going to be a wedding in Acorn Falls! When Katie's mom announces plans to remarry, Katie learns that she's also getting a step-brother.

STAR QUALITY

☆17 When Sabrina's favorite game show comes to Acorn Falls, she's determined to get on the show, *and* get her friends to be part of her act.

KEEPING THE BEAT

☆18 Randy's band Iron Wombat is more popular than ever after winning the Battle of the Bands. But Randy's excitement turns sour when the band is booked for Stacy the great's birthday bash!

LOOK FOR THE GIRL TALK SERIES!
IN A STORE NEAR YOU!

TALK BACK!

TELL US WHAT YOU THINK ABOUT GIRL TALK

Name _____

Address _____

City _____ State _____ Zip _____

Birthday Day _____ Mo. _____ Year _____

Telephone Number (___) _____

1) On a scale of 1 (The Pits) to 5 (The Max),
how would you rate Girl Talk?   Circle One:

         1   2   3   4   5

2) What do you like most about Girl Talk?

___Characters___Situations___Telephone Talk

Other _____

3) Who is your favorite character? Circle One:

    Sabrina   Katie   Randy

    Allison   Stacy   Other

4) Who is your least favorite character?

_____

5) What do you want to read about in Girl Talk?

_____

_____

Send completed form to :
Western Publishing Company, Inc.
1220 Mound Avenue Mail Station #85
Racine, Wisconsin 53404